TWO

TWO

A Novel

GULZAR

INTRODUCTION BY PAVAN K. VARMA

HARPER**PERENNIAL**

First published in hardback in India in 2017 by Harper Perennial
An imprint of HarperCollins *Publishers* India
A-75, Sector 57, Noida, Uttar Pradesh 201301, India
www.harpercollins.co.in

2 4 6 8 10 9 7 5 3 1

P-ISBN: 978-93-5177-520-1
E-ISBN: 978-93-5177-521-8

Typeset in 12/16 Adobe Garamond Pro at
SÜRYA, New Delhi

Printed and bound at
Thomson Press (India) Ltd

To
Sardar Makhan Singh
and
Sujaan Kaur
of
Dina. Pakistan.

CONTENTS

FOREWORD

This novel was originally written in Urdu. That's my medium of writing. But then, it included many words and phrases in Punjabi, Saraiki and other dialects spoken in that area of Punjab which became Pakistan after Partition. I belong to that area. I was born in Dina, in the city of Jhelum, which is pronounced 'Jehlum' colloquially.

Translating the novel into English became a bit of a hurdle.

Sukrita Paul, a dear friend, took it upon herself to do it. But I was not at ease while reading it. Shantanu Ray Chaudhuri, another friend, tried to improve on it. Being a professional editor and writer in English, he did the job well. But still I was not at ease.

It didn't read like it read in Urdu, blending the tones and dialects I had used in the narrative.

I put the novel away for a while.

A lot has been written about the Partition. Sukrita herself has done a lot of work on the subject, and authored a book, *Translating Partition*. Her father, the celebrated Urdu writer Joginder Paul, had experienced the Partition and written a lot about it. So had I.

But in this novel, I wished to examine the status of the refugees after the Partition. It took them decades to settle down and come to terms with the haunting memories. In fact, that process of settling down is still going on. Seventy years have passed.

So, I took up the novel again and decided to work on the translation myself. You may not find 'perfect' or 'proper' English in it, but you will find stories of refugees, and how life planted them all over the world. A lot of Sukrita's translated lines have remained in this. So have those of Shantanu's.

I am still not at ease with this.

But then, I wanted this to be over as we complete seventy years of the Partition, this year, in 2017.

GULZAR

INTRODUCTION

Imagine a compellingly chiselled poem expanded to become a story in prose. Or, imagine the opposite, a story compressed with such refined elegance that it becomes a poem. Or, take even a third alternative: a screenplay that could, if expanded, become a novel, and, if condensed, is transmuted into a poem.

Gulzar's first attempt at a longer work of fiction is all three in one: a poem, a screenplay, a novel. It is a poem because the imagery reads like one; it is a screenplay because each episode is like a picture unfolding before your eyes; and it is a novel because it tells a story in a format that is neither a poem nor a screenplay.

Gulzar Saheb has often joked with me that he wished he could write a 'full-length' novel like I wrote once. I am glad that he hasn't tried to. The reason for this is simple: his new work is of just the right length, longer than a short story, and shorter than a full-fledged novel. In doing so, it retains the dramatic brevity of a short story, but has the texture of a novel.

A novella has been the subject of much literary scrutiny. It somehow defies conventional categorization, but in this very act of creative defiance lies the secret of its intense impact. The genre is not new. Munshi Premchand wrote several. So did Albert Camus (*The Stranger*), Ernest Hemingway (*The Old Man and the Sea*) and George Orwell (*Animal Farm*), to mention but a few examples.

A work of fiction is a work of fiction. Its size does not matter, so long as its impact and quality are indubitable. Why should the number of pages determine the quality of literary expression? Who decides how long a work of fiction should be? Should a story end when the reader is yearning for it to continue, or should it last till the reader begins to wonder when it will end? Fiction that is a tome is legitimate if it holds the attention of the reader; similarly, fiction that is shorter is equally valid if it keeps the reader enthralled. Limitations of any kind to the canvas of creative expression are arbitrary impositions of critics. The key question is whether the story being rendered is complete enough, whatever its length, to convey in a gripping manner the theme animating the writer.

In his book *Different Seasons*, a collection of four novellas, Stephen King called the novella 'an ill-defined and disreputable banana republic'. Perhaps, it was an act of overstated and deliberate self-deprecation, because his readers found them as readable as ever. On the other hand, the Irish writer Ian McEwan wrote in *The New Yorker* (12 October 2012) that 'the novella is the perfect form of prose fiction'. It retains focus, moves at a faster pace, covers the same canvas as a novel but with far greater intensity, brings in necessary details but cuts out the unnecessary factual meanderings, and allows characters to blossom while omitting the verbal flab. It is as readable as a novel and, arguably, more satisfying than a short story. In other words, it is the perfect literary modus vivendi, offering to the reader a novel that is shorter than a work of fiction that is too long, and a work of fiction that is as satisfying as a novel but not too short.

Of course, as is true of all literary genres, the success of the novella depends not on the nature of its structure alone, but far more importantly, on the literary dexterity of the person who writes it. When Gulzar embraces the format, the novella has met a truly consummate partner. As proof, one has only to read *Two*.

Two is about the Partition of 1947, a cataclysmically tragic event that Gulzar lived through. Even as Independence drew nearer, British cartographers worked overtime to draw the boundaries of two nations, one India, the other Pakistan. What was one land became two, separated by an unbridgeable gap that made millions refugees overnight. Some ten to fifteen million people – men, women, children, young and old – were displaced by a destiny they did not choose. It is estimated that some two million lost their lives in the frenzied bloodbath that accompanied this division.

Time erases wounds, but memories remain, like smouldering embers below the ash even when the fires of history appear to have died. *Two* is about those memories, those embers, recalled through a story that transports you to the agonies and dilemmas of ordinary people, both Hindus and Muslims, who suffered as a consequence of the Partition.

It is written in Gulzar's inimitable – and riveting – style. The narrative, involving a bunch of characters who could be you or me or people we know, unfolds, scene by scene, in a manner that brings the traumatic days leading up to 1947 vibrantly – even painfully – alive. Each character is unique, and will remain etched in our minds, not by the length of the description, but by the writer's ability to make the portrayal come alive through just a flourish of linguistic colour, a trait, a gesture, an expression, a situation, a dialogue, or even an abuse.

But *Two* does not end with the Partition. It carries us along, to decades later, where, in the strangest ways, the strands that unravelled in 1947 come together. In that journey, the 1984 riots against the Sikhs become a metaphor for the continuance of hate and violence in societies. The same emotions that made the Partition one of the most gory chapters of India's modern history are now repeated in entirely different circumstances, only to prove the point that the irrational and warped furies that lurk just below the surface of 'civilized' societies can be easily triggered even when the past should have taught us to overcome them resolutely.

Gulzar Saheb's debut as a novelist is a spectacular one. *Two* is unputdownable because the narrative is in the hands of a craftsman for whom words are like clay in the hands of a master potter. Gulzar writes with the eye of a sensitive film-maker, the feel of a poet, and the touch of one who has himself been singed for life by the story he narrates. Long after we put the book down, the characters, and the series of events in which they become pawns in the sweep of history, continue to haunt us. One continues to read the book long after having finished its last page.

PAVAN K. VARMA

Part One

Master Fazal would say…

'History is on the rampage, making giant strides. It's happening right in front of us. The Second World War ended and Germany was broken into two pieces – East Germany and West Germany. The country was divided, but then it divided the people too. Earlier, they were one people, now they are two.

'Six crore thirty lakh people lost their lives for this.'

In Campbellpur, people would gather around him – like in a chaupal … a long pipe of a gurgling hookah would keep changing hands.

Master Fazal added this time, 'Another giant step of history is about to fall here – in Hindustan. Some forces are contemplating another partition, of land and people. Hindustan is to be divided into two and a new country named Pakistan to be created.

'Once again, millions of lives will be at stake.'

A hush fell on the gathering.

'A million?' Nabi whispered as he took a long drag from the hookah.

He passed on the pipe to Master Fazal, who took a longer and deeper drag. People waited for his next comment.

Master Fazal cleared his throat before passing the pipe to Rahman.

'This arrogant, conceited history strides ahead with her head in the clouds and never looks down. She does not realize how she crushes millions of people beneath her feet. The common people. She doesn't understand that one may cut a mountain in two, but people? It's a hard task, Bhai, to cut one people into two. They bleed.'

Campbellpur was as much a city as a qasba. Not quite a well-knit city, but sprawling clusters. Rather like pockets stitched into a coat. There's a settlement on its outskirts, close to the highway, much like a sleeve of that coat, referred to as the adda. Trucks moved in and out of the basti the whole day, keeping the fire in the dhabas burning. When they drove away, life in the basti would settle down. People would hang around in small groups. Some belonged to this basti, others were small-time traders from nearby towns.

The year was 1946. The country had not yet been divided, but people had begun to drift apart. Passing trucks left some rumours hanging, while city folk too added their own wings to them. It all began at a dhaba in Campbellpur, the dark shack at the back of Lakhbeera's dhaba.

Fauji hollered at Hameed, 'M'hidya, hand me a soda!'

At times, Fauji needed the soda just to get the bitter drink down his throat. Lakhbeera, the owner of the dhaba, would send for another plate of liver. Hameed, his trusted aide who managed the dhaba, would rush to deliver. Fauji and Lakhbeera were thick as thieves. Fauji did not get along with anyone else. They would drink for hours, sitting by the one-eyed window – one of its panes was broken while the others remained shut. It offered Lakhbeera the only glimpse of the adda outside.

Lakhbeera gulped the drunk and said, 'This fellow, Painti-Chhatti, always leaves behind some provocative news, yaar!' Painti-Chhatti, or 3536, was the owner of a truck and was always referred to by its number.

Fauji talked very little. His eyes scanned the room like a torch in the dark as he poured the soda into his drink.

Lakhbeera was itching to spit out some news, but Fauji did not encourage him. He knew what

Lakhbeera wanted to say. Nowadays, gossip smouldered everywhere.

Fauji was not really an army man. There was nothing fauji-like about him. Maybe it was his khaki jacket that got him the name. He wore it day in and day out. A dozen buttons shone on the front – that is why he had bought it. Though he never washed the jacket, he kept those buttons gleaming. Like his gleaming eyes. He had sharp eyes which retained all that he saw.

Unable to hold back any longer, Lakhbeera blurted out, 'Painti-Chhatti was saying that Musalmans stripped Hindu women and paraded them naked in Sheikhupura.'

Fauji remained silent.

'Why?' Lakhbeera raged. 'Are all the Khalsas dead?'

Fauji's eyes recorded this too.

Lakhbeera took a sip, swallowing the news with it. 'Don't Muslims have mothers and sisters?' he muttered. 'F*** Painti-Chhatti's sister!'

Rumours gradually became news. And the news began to ferment. People believed whatever they heard.

Someone said, 'Musalmans have abducted Tiwari's daughter-in-law!'

'Tiwari must have got it done himself! He has been wanting this for long.'

'What is his problem with her?' Pali enquired.

'She is a widow. Tiwari's son died four years ago. His grandson is five years old.'

'So?' Pritpal pouted.

'The girl wanted to take her son away. To her parents.'

'So?'

'Tiwari did not want to part with his grandchild. One night, the mother-in-law threw her out of the house.'

'So?'

'She spent the night in Sheikh Umar's house. It's he who brought her back in the morning.'

A long pause followed before Pali asked again, 'So?'

'F*** your "so", shut up now!'

After another pause, Pritpal spoke once again: 'So where was I that night?'

There was an explosion of laughter.

Campbellpur had yet another pocket. This was deep in the city, and thickly populated. Someone shot off a rumour in M.B. Middle School that the day Pakistan is created, all Hindus would have to vacate their homes and leave for Hindustan.

'Why?' inquired Master Karam Singh.

'Because Muslims coming from Hindustan will need houses to live in. Where else will they live? On the roads?'

Master Karam Singh had never been able to comprehend political issues. And when he could not understand something, he had one recourse: Master Fazal.

His faith in Master Fazal was as strong as it was in the Guru Granth Sahib. Karam Singh would often say, 'Oye, he has read it all. He knows them all, all the bhagats of Granth Sahib: Bhagat Kabir, Bhagat Namdev, Bhagat Farid, Bhagat Bulleh Shah ... he can recite them all.'

Karam Singh and Fazaldeen were old friends. Both taught at the Middle School. Fazal taught history and Karam Singh, arithmetic. The headmaster was some Anglo-Indian. His name suggested that he was south Indian, Stephen Menon. He had converted from Santosh Menon to Stephen Menon. Though Fazaldeen was junior headmaster, he wielded the authority of the senior headmaster. Menon was a science teacher, but since he was often away in Lahore, Master Fazaldeen would end up taking his classes.

'Oye, why do you take his burden for no reason? He spends half the year in L'hore anyway.'

'His dark-skinned mem lives there in Lahore, Karme. She has a big accommodation there … given by the government. She too is a teacher, na.'

'What does she teach?'

'Bible! Don't you know they hold Bible classes in missionary schools?'

'Oye, to hell with him and his mem! Let him share half his salary with you!'

Fazlu master had the habit of rumbling the hookah like a Chaudhri. After a puff or two, he smiled.

'Karmu … you won't understand. You are, after all, a sardar. You'll get it a little later.'

'Okay, explain it to me.'

'See, I have started to understand some fundamental formulae after reading his science books. Have you heard of Rash Behari Bose?'

'Yes, yes. The Bengali rebel! The one who hurled a bomb at the white people.'

'Did he get the bomb from Japan?' asked Fazal.

'No, no – he made it himself, he and that other one ... the Allahabad guy, what's his name ... Chandra Shekhar...'

'So, if we don't teach science to our children, how will another Azad and Bhagat Singh emerge? How will we get independence? Let Menon go to hell. My purpose is to prepare these children...'

Fazaldeen's voice fell to a whisper.

Karam Singh's eyes opened in wonder. Inserting a finger into his turban, he kept trying to cajole his ears out. Now, banging a hand on Master Fazaldeen's, he shouted in a full-throated voice: 'Zindabad, my very own yaar, Fazlu!'

He was so loud that Fazlu's begum came rushing. Both the sons also peeped in from behind. Fazlu quickly brought the situation under control.

'No, no, all's well! My yaar Karmu gets excited at times. Get another glass of sharbat for him.'

As soon as his wife left, Fazlu tried to explain yet again, in a whisper. 'These matters need to be kept under wraps. They are not to be announced. In fact, even one's own thoughts should not be heard.'

'Fazaldeen, you know me.' Now Karam Singh's voice too became a whisper. 'I keep your words locked in my heart. No one will get even a whiff!' He moved closer to Fazaldeen and whispered, 'Oye, can you make a bomb?'

It hadn't been long since they had exchanged these words ... yet by 1946 nobody thought about them anymore. They had been covered in dust and grime.

Europe was aflame. The Second World War scorched its lands, spewed cinders. No part of the world was left unscathed, and Hindustan was flailing for its independence. Freedom campaigns were gathering momentum ... and Master Fazal thought it was quite futile to be teaching about Henry the First or Henry the Second in his history class. These were not times to entertain children with the adventures of Robinson Crusoe. While teaching history, Fazal would invariably drift into explaining the context of the war. Both the sparks of war as well as the embers of his desire for independence burned in his heart.

'It's not politics I am talking about. It's simple ... if the Hindustani army goes to fight on behalf of...'

He paused, stopped himself from saying 'the British', and said, '...the Allied forces, it will be an army of slaves of the British. If they are independent, they could be fighting for their friends. But it must be ascertained who amongst the Allied forces are friends and who enemies. Subhash-babu...' He halted several times as he talked. As far as the British were concerned, Subhash-babu was an enemy because he had aligned with Hitler. For Master Fazal, he was the hero of the freedom struggle.

One day, in class, he inadvertently said, 'Subhash-babu had urged us, "Give me blood and I'll give you freedom."'

Children were excited and shouted, 'Subhash-babu Zindabad!' They had often heard this slogan. The headmaster, Stephen Menon, summoned Master Fazal to his office.

Soon, Master Fazal's house was raided. It was rumoured that some bomb-making tools were recovered, though no bomb was found.

The police filed a case. To set an example to the students of the school, the British officer tied him to an easel and got him whipped in the school ground.

It was quite a sight.

Master Fazal was tied to the easel in the middle of the ground. The whole school, teachers and students, gathered around. A British officer circled him on horseback. Policemen stood at short distances, their rifles at the ready. A whip lashed his naked back at every command of the officer.

'Keep whipping him till the sun sets,' ordered the gora and galloped out of the school grounds.

At that moment, Master Karam Singh emerged from the crowd, screaming. He rushed to shield Master Fazal, bearing the brunt of the lashes himself.

Suddenly, the congregation erupted in chaos. Everybody leapt forward. The police fired in the air. In the melee, Karam Singh pulled Master Fazal down from the easel and fled, carrying him on his back. He ran into the back lane and knocked on the door of a house that belonged to one of his students. He hid Fazal there.

For many days after, the police made the rounds of his house in search of Fazlu. Karam Singh would mark attendance on his behalf at the police station. Though the police found no evidence against him and the case was dismissed, Master Fazal was suspended from the school. He had to keep reporting to the police. They would summon him as and when they pleased. Sometimes, it was at Inspector Sharma's order, other times, Verma's. Both were stooges of the British. They tried to link him to any untoward incident that took place.

Master Fazal had two sons. Both of them studied in the same school. In addition to paying their fees, Master Karam Singh organized some tuitions for Fazlu. Students came over to Fazlu's house to study. His friendship with Karam Singh deepened. Such was the nature of their relationship that neither were there any obligations nor any overt show of gratitude. However, the call for Pakistan embroiled them in a debate.

Master Fazal talked with wisdom and knowledge of history, while Karam Singh picked up information from newspapers. Karam Singh knew only what he read and what he heard.

'Oye, listen, Fazlu, is the country a slate that

Jinnah can break? Is it a slate we can divide between you and me? Does a country break? Oye, Hindustan is one country, na? It's one land, how can it be broken?' Karam Singh was a very sentimental man.

Master Fazal then raised some questions that baffled Karam Singh.

'Okay, tell me, Karme. Remember that land, the one owned by Deendayal? Don't know how many acres. Wasn't that divided? Divided into three parts: two parts went to the two sons and one was left for him.'

'But that was a division of the family, Fazaldeen! The land did not break into two!'

'This is the same, Karme. Jinnah is talking about the division of the country, not breaking the land.'

Somewhat shaken, Karam Singh said, 'But why, yaar? I have not done anything, nor have you! Why should our land be divided?'

Gradually, Pakistan began to emerge on the map. It was clear now that Pakistan would have to be created.

Once, Karam Singh innocently asked, 'Fazlu, tell

me something. If Pakistan is created, will you leave me and go away to Pakistan?' He did not know that Pakistan was to be created right there, where he lived. When Fazal Master explained which areas were to go to Pakistan, Karam Singh smiled and said, 'No worries then. First, there were the British. Now my own yaar will rule over me!'

But when someone declared that Hindus and Sikhs would have to vacate their houses when Muslims migrated from Hindustan, Karam Singh was taken aback. To understand this new issue, he turned to Fazlu.

Master Fazlu asked Karam Singh, 'Why would the Muslims come from Hindustan?'

'I never asked that stupid fellow!'

'Karme, this is like the issue of Deendayal's farm. Nobody is going to lift his land and carry it elsewhere. The land will remain where it is. Only those who till the land will be divided into two. Those who harvest it will be divided. The division takes place because one of them denies the rights of the other. Now, he cannot do so…'

'Okay, what's the problem then? Why are people

screaming that the country has been partitioned? That it has been divided. You tell me, do you want Pakistan? If it's good for you, I will surely fight for your rights. My yaar wants Pakistan. All right then, Pakistan Zindabad! Tell me, do you want Pakistan?'

Master Fazaldeen lowered his eyes. He was unable to answer. He was unable to say: 'These Sharmas and Vermas are after my life and even call me a "sulla". They humiliate us. That's why Muslims want Pakistan!'

Sometimes, Master Fazal offered amazing explanations. Master Karam Singh would say, 'He has big eyes, he is the wide, open sky, the whole of it. He sees it all.'

People were sitting on the rooftop, newspapers wrapped around their hand. Master Fazal was saying...

'History is on the rampage, making giant strides. It's happening right in front of us. The Second World War ended and Germany was broken into two pieces – East Germany and West Germany. The country was divided, but then it divided the people too. Earlier, they were one people, now they are two.

'Six crore thirty lakh people lost their lives for this.'

In Campbellpur, people would gather around him – like in a chaupal … a long pipe of a gurgling hookah would keep changing hands.

Master Fazal added this time, 'Another giant step of history is about to fall here – in Hindustan. Some forces are contemplating another partition, of land and people. Hindustan is to be divided into two and a new country named Pakistan created.

'Once again, millions of lives will be at stake.'

A hush fell on the gathering.

'A million?' Nabi whispered as he took a long drag from the hookah.

He passed on the pipe to Master Fazal, who took a longer and deeper drag. People waited for his next comment.

Master Fazal cleared his throat before passing the pipe to Rahman.

'This arrogant, conceited history strides ahead with her head in the clouds and never looks down.

She does not realize how she crushes millions of people beneath her feet. The common people. She doesn't understand that one may cut a mountain in two, but people? It's a hard task, Bhai to cut one people into two. They bleed.'

A deep sigh coursed through the gathering. Master Fazal said, 'History will keep on marching like this. The names of a few people will stick to her fabric. She will register those. There was Hitler, there was Mussolini, Churchill and Joseph Stalin, among others. This time, the names may be Mahatma Gandhi, Jawaharlal Nehru, Jinnah, Subhash Bose! But the names of all the lakhs and crores who have lost their lives will be nowhere. They will be mere numbers in which all of us will be included!'

This time, Fazaldeen took a long breath and said, 'That is how this arrogant history walks with her head held high. She doesn't deign to look down and see what she crushes beneath her feet. Doesn't see that there are people below!'

A piece of meat was stuck in the cavity of Fauji's teeth. He was trying to pull it out with matchsticks that were piling up, broken, on the table. His gums started bleeding.

Lakhbeera said, 'Let it be, it will come out on its own. After all, it's just a piece of meat. If it doesn't come out, it will go in.'

Pritpal was sitting with them. He said, 'This is like Tiwari's daughter-in-law. She is neither welcome in the family, nor thrown out.'

Fauji had heard the story and looked at him, his eyes flashing. 'Why are you obsessed with that lady?' they seemed to say.

Pritpal looked away at once, picked up the glass and gulped down the drink, got up and left.

Suddenly, there were loud sounds right outside the one-eyed window.

Blurting out an abuse, Lakhbeera said: 'It's that f***ing Painti-Chhatti. He must have brought some provocative news again.'

Painti-Chhatti had indeed brought disturbing news. 'Musalmans have thrown a cow's head into a Krishna mandir in Mirpur! Riots have erupted in the city. Hindus are running away, abandoning their homes.'

'Where are they running off to?' somebody asked.

'Towards Hindustan.'

'So where are we? We are in Hindustan, after all. Pakistan hasn't been created yet.'

'But it will be formed soon, it seems.'

'Who knows where it will be formed. This side or the other side. Is there a place where there are no Muslims?'

Pakistan had begun to take shape in the minds of the people. Only the declaration was awaited. It looked like there was no going back on the partition now. Even if the leaders wanted to turn the clock back, it was no longer possible. Anyone who tried would be killed.

Those who had hoped the partition would not happen used to say, 'Bapu will not allow it. Pakistan will be created on Bapu's dead body or, if it happens, Bapu will drop dead.' Those who feared losing their homes did not want the partition. Those who knew they could remain where they were, were ready for it.

The seeds sown by the British had sprouted thorns which had begun to prick. They were masters of their craft. If Fazal was being hounded by a Verma or a Sharma, Rai Bahadur had a Rahim or a Karim after him. A case had been filed against Rai Bahadur Des Raj, who had a relationship with Panna Bai, the kothe-wali. It was alleged that he had killed Usman Pathan with the help of an English officer named Gary Tomson. Usman had called Panna Bai his concubine and made claims over her earnings. It appears that Gary had a scuffle with Usman after a drink or two, and shot him with a revolver. The revolver belonged to Rai Bahadur. Gary's ordeal ended with him migrating to England, but Rai Bahadur was left fielding the case. He now had to appear before either Inspector Rahimullah or Sub-inspector Karimullah.

Rai Bahadur used to wear a Pathani turban over a golden 'kulla'. A silk shirt with a starched cotton shalwar was his regular dress. He looked every inch a nawab. Inspector Rahim resented that. The first thing he would do whenever Rai Bahadur reported to him was to make him remove his turban and keep it on the table. He mocked him, 'Wear a topi, Lala, a topi. This turban is for Pathans, not for lalas!'

If he had his way, Rai Bahadur would have shot

both of them. Rahim as well as Karim! But the goras who could help him were on their way out. On his way back from the police station, he would go to Panna's kotha to get over the trauma. In a way, she was also obliged to him. It was because of him she could save whatever she earned. Otherwise, Usman would have left her with nothing.

She was the daughter of mirasis. Usman had seen her at a wedding, singing. He enticed her and eloped with her from Amritsar. Got her to recite the Kalma and made her go through a sham nikaah. Alcoholic and debauched as he was, the home soon became a kotha. Usman had another house. In Peshawar, where his wife and two young sons lived. Once, he took Panna Bai there. He got such a thrashing from his father-in-law, he came running back. After this, all earnings from his in-laws ceased and Panna became his sole provider.

Rai Bahadur sat facing Karimullah. The turban lay to a side. Karimullah asked, 'Lala-ji, now that the English are leaving, why not return the title of Rai Bahadur? What value will it have after they leave?'

'Let them leave. It will come off on its own. It's

only because I am Rai Bahadur that you ask me to sit. Or else you'd keep me standing!'

Karimullah broke into a laugh and said, 'How long, Lala-ji! This case too will go away on its own. Neither will you be here nor will I have any queries.'

'Why?' Rai Bahadur asked. 'Where will I go and why won't you ask questions?'

'You won't be here once Pakistan is created. You will go away to your country.'

He did not say 'Hindustan'.

Rai Bahadur asked, 'If Pakistan is created, will you people turn us out?'

Rahimullah entered the room. He replied, 'Why would we turn you out, Lala-ji? You are our neighbours, our countrymen. But with all the killings in your country, will the people here remain quiet? If they lose their head, how long can we protect you?'

Des Raj gaped at him, speechless.

Karim got up and Rahim took his seat.

Before Pakistan took shape on the map, it started taking shape in the minds of the people. This was true of both Hindus and Muslims. The untouchables had been similarly alienated centuries ago. This time, it was not the wells and the temples but the land itself that was separated. A division that split identities.

As the year 1946 approached its end, the borders of the partition started emerging. As the date of independence came closer, freedom seemed to move further away.

That very evening, when Rai Bahadur dropped in at Panna's, she was not home. People no longer visited the place as often as they used to. He was greeted by Shamima, the maid. Whenever Rai Bahadur visited, he carried his whiskey in a silver pocket flask. Shamima always made his drink from it.

'Where is she?' asked Rai Bahadur.

'She didn't tell me.' Shamima took the silver flask from him and went inside. Rai Bahadur reclined on the divan.

'This hasn't happened before. She never goes anywhere at this time of the day.'

Shamima brought him his drink. She sat a little distance away, resting her back against a door.

'The city is drying up, Rai Sahib. I feel I should

go back to my village. I am here only for the sake of this girl. Otherwise, she will be left alone.'

Rai Bahadur turned over to his side against the bolster. 'Where will you go?'

'I'll go to P'shor. Usman brought me from there.'

Des Raj sighed. 'Everyone is talking about leaving. One can feel the tremors on the earth's surface – waiting to erupt the moment one steps on it.'

Just then, Jamil Miya turned up. 'Arre bhai, where is Panna? Doesn't she sit in the Diwankhana anymore?'

Shamima shook her head.

Jamil Miya said, 'Well, a friend from Britain is visiting and I thought I'll have him entertained. Shall I bring him over? Or shall I take her? But where has she gone?'

'I don't know,' said Shamima.

'Okay. Bring me some paan.'

Shamima was unable to refuse. After all, he was an old patron. She went in to prepare the paan. Jamil turned to Rai Bahadur. 'Achha, Rai Bahadur, tell me – will Lahore remain here or will it go to the other side?'

'Where will it go? It will remain where it is.'

Jamil laughed. 'Wonderful!'

Shamima returned. Jamil put some coins on the tray, took the paan and left.

Rai Bahadur took a long deep breath and muttered, 'Even lines have begun to be drawn now.'

That evening, Panna went to see Fauji at the adda.

Fauji drove Ujagar Singh's trucks. Ujagar Singh lived somewhere in old Delhi but often visited Campbellpur on work. Though Fauji was an employee, he also had a share in Ujagar Singh's business. That's why he enjoyed a different status amongst the truck drivers. At some point, he had been friends with Usman Khan. He used to get crates of Scotch whiskey for Usman from the cantonment at concessional rates and deliver them at the kotha. That was where he first met Panna. He always treated her as Usman's wife, and was a man of great integrity. He said little but held firmly to what he said.

Panna had come with what remained of her savings and jewellery, all tied in a little bundle. Fauji was getting himself a massage on the rooftop. He sent the masseur away the moment she arrived and pulled the khes over his tehmad before he sat down. When Panna opened her bundle, he was startled.

'What are you up to? Why have you brought all these to me?'

'Please take me to my parents.'

'Parents…?'

'If only I could go back to the soil I came from. Here, I found neither home, nor my motherland! I have brought whatever is left with me. Take me to the place from where Usman uprooted me … my roots lie scattered, broken.'

'Are you mad, Panna? Is this any time to travel anywhere? Haven't you heard of all the chaos in the country? You know Ujagar Singh, don't you, my boss and partner … lives that side. In Dilli. He is stuck there. No news, no letter. Post offices are closed … trains are stranded. I hear, some go halfway and return, while others come halfway and go back…'

'That's why I have come to you. You keep going to Amritsar.'

'I go up to Ludhiana or Jullundur too. If only there were some way out!'

Silence lingered between them for a while. Fauji slowly tied the bundle and handed it back to her, placing his hand over hers.

'Don't worry. If I go, I will definitely take you along … even if I have to take you in potato sacks. Keep this money. It will be useful there if not here.'

As he stood up, the tehmad threatened to slip. 'Oye f***—' He grabbed at it.

Panna turned her eyes away and left.

The axe fell right in the middle and the log split into two.

Master Karam Singh stood in his courtyard, chopping wood. His turban had slid down to his neck. His daughter-in-law came out of the kitchen and said, 'Bhapa-ji, why are you cutting so much wood? There's enough.'

'Never mind. It'll come handy.'

After a while, tired, he rested the axe against a wall and started to tie his turban properly. Ever since the schools had closed, it was difficult to pass the time. Avtar, his elder son, had gone to meet his sister's in-laws four villages away. At Derewalan. That is where Karam Singh's daughter Nikki had been married. Avtar had also taken his mother along. He was to have returned in three or four hours. They may have stopped for lunch, but now evening was upon them.

Avtar's wife, Satya, saw Master-ji's concern in his furrowed brow. He was cutting the wood not just to while away time, but to dispel his anxiety. She too was anxious, but there was nothing she could do.

She said, 'Even Bhuri keeps looking at the entrance. He feeds her every day before she is milked.'

Master-ji grunted. 'He will come, Bhuriye! Avtar must be on his way now!'

In response, when the buffalo mooed loudly, he said: 'Look, she has started calling out his name. You don't call him by his name, but this one does!'

A ripple of laughter passed between them, leaving their hearts no lighter. They were trying to reassure each other. Karam Singh said, taking a dig at his wife, 'See, if he had been alone on his cycle, he would have been here by now. But he has carried along a two-ton sack.'

Bahu protested, 'But Beeji is not that fat.'

'What do you know, bitiya, how heavy she is! Come, hand me the bucket, I'll milk the buffalo.'

'Bhapa-ji, have you ever lifted Beeji?' Bahu asked, washing the bucket.

'What do you know! I'd lift her on my shoulders and do the bhangra when we were young.'

Bahu brought him the bucket. He washed the udder of the buffalo and began milking. In the meantime, Satya peeped out into the lane echoing all the way with hushed whispers.

She said, almost to herself but within his earshot, 'Some really bad news from Montgomery!'

'About the riots? It's nothing ... Only rumours!'

The first stream of milk fell into the bucket like the ringing of a bell. A crease appeared on Master-ji's forehead.

'I had told your mother-in-law ... Let Avtar go alone ... he'll bring back news about his sister and her family. But she just doesn't listen to anyone.'

He was growing angrier with his wife by the minute.

'The other day when I wanted to go there myself, she wouldn't let me.'

Satya tried to reassure him. 'They will come back soon, Bhapa-ji. Why do you worry?'

Just then, there was a thud in the lane outside. Perhaps it was Phajju's bullock cart. Soon it came and halted in front of the door. When Satya's face flushed red, it became apparent how pale it had been a little earlier. Avtar Singh was getting his cycle down from the cart. Master-ji spoke from where he sat milking the buffalo.

'Oye, what took you so long?'

Phajju shouted his greeting from the door: 'Salaam alaikum, Master-ji!'

'Walekum-as-salaam, Bhai Phajju. Come, have a couple of milk streams. Have a glassful before you go.'

'Some other time, Master-ji. I'm in a hurry … Veer-ji's cycle got punctured on the way. Good that we met. Okay then, Allah beli!'

When Phajju had left, Master-ji asked Avtar, 'Oye, where have you left your bebe? I don't see her.'

'She'll stay there for a day or two. Nikki's mother-in-law insisted.'

Avtar Singh began to wash his hands and feet under the tap. Satya hung his clothes and a towel close by. A strange silence enveloped the courtyard.

Master-ji put out the fodder for the buffalo, kept the milk in the kitchen and asked, 'What news? From the Derewalans.'

Avtar walked across the yard and said, 'It doesn't look very good, Bhapa-ji!'

'Why? Has something happened there?'

'Not really, but…'

He paused and Master-ji said, irritated, 'Oye, these are mere rumours. Just rumours. They fly around like bats.'

'If they are mere rumours, why did Stephen Menon close the school and run away? In the middle of the night, he called for a military truck and escaped.'

'That Anglo-Indian was bound to feel threatened… He belongs neither to India nor England. Where will he go after the British leave? He was the one who had Master Fazaldeen whipped in the school. His skin peeled off. His blood still stains my back. Who will run away if not he?'

Avtar fell silent.

After muttering something to himself, Master-ji said, 'It's been days since I last met Fazlu. People in his lane have started looking at me with suspicion.'

Campbellpur was now simmering like a pot with a fire underneath – it had begun to rumble and smoke. Sometimes, when people heard of a fire somewhere, they climbed the rooftops to check. At least half of the city was visible from those rooftops, as were the many radio aerials.

Umar Sheikh had a radio. Its aerial was fixed to a bamboo stick he had propped up on the roof of his house, which was at the end of Master Karam Singh's lane. There was a time when Umar Sheikh would have the courtyard sprinkled with water during summer and sit down to smoke his hookah. At times, he would call out to Master-ji when the latter walked past his house.

'Master-ji, your school gets the newspaper every

day, which they discard every evening. Please bring it here for me to read,' he would say.

'But you have a radio. You listen to the news every day. Why would you want to read stale news?'

'The newspaper confirms whether what is said on the radio is true ... It can say anything...'

'How is that possible? After all, it belongs to the government.'

'Damn the government! After the whites leave, they won't be able to manage.'

When the radio was switched on at six in the evening for four hours, one did not feel like believing the kind of news it delivered.

Master-ji said, 'Then call me when the news airs. Even I'd like to know what the government has to say.'

But that never happened. Sheikh never called him, nor did Master-ji ever go over. And now, Umar Sheikh had even stopped sitting outside.

Tired of listening to all kinds of sickening news from his son and daughter-in-law, Karam Singh went knocking at Umar Sheikh's door one day. To listen to the news. Sheikh Sahib answered the door. 'Come, come in, Sardar-ji.'

He seated Karam Singh in the living room with great respect and asked, 'What can I serve you?'

'Sheikh Sahib, I have come here to listen to your radio. This is perhaps the time for news.'

'But the radio is not working today. Some fuse has blown.'

'O ho ... I thought...'

Just then some sounds could be heard from within. 'Do you have some guests?' he asked, rising.

Sheikh Sahib responded hastily, 'Meera is here from Meerut.'

'Oh ... bitiya has come after many years! Can I meet her? Why should there be any purdah from the father?'

Just as he stepped forward, Sheikh Sahib stopped him.

'No, not yet. She's not too well.'

'What's the matter with her? Did you call Hakim Sahib? Shall I get him?'

Sheikh Sahib's eyes welled up with tears.

'No, no, Sardar-ji...'

'What's the matter, Sheikh Sahib?' Karam Singh asked, placing a hand on Umar Sheikh's.

Sheikh Sahib broke down.

'Meera's husband was killed ... in the riots ... at Meerut.'

Master Karam Singh's legs trembled as he walked out. He took a few steps, staggered and fell.

That night, Master-ji did not have dinner. He went to the terrace and lay down. When Satya came to call him, he turned the other side.

'I am not hungry.'

After a while, Avtar approached him. 'What's the matter, Bhapa-ji?'

'Listen, beta. How will your bebe return? Who will go to fetch her?'

'Jeeja-ji said he will bring her. Maybe Nikki will come too. She's expecting, na!'

'I see...' Master-ji fell silent.

What was once spoken of in hushed whispers could now be seen. Someone had set fire to Lakhbeera's shack. Or maybe it caught fire just like that. It was inflammable, after all. But it burned down for no reason. The entire city held its breath. Everyone sat with their hearts in their mouths. And there was not even a rumour to offset the tension.

Lakhbeera was a Sikh. Footloose and fancy free. A vagrant. His parents lived in Rawalpindi. He was in school when he ran away from home after a quarrel with his stepmother. His house was close to a toll booth where the trucks going out of the city queued up at night. Lakhbeera hid in a truck full of sacks. When the truck halted at a dhaba in Campbellpur, the driver spotted him. He asked the boy to get down and discovered that he was from 'Pindi. Khan, the truck driver, left him with the dhaba owner, promising to pick him up on his way back. Lakhbeera worked at the dhaba for a few days.

One day at the dhaba, the boy came across his picture in an Urdu newspaper. His parents were trying to find him. That day, he cut his hair short. And before Khan returned, Lakhbeera befriended another truck driver and left with him as a cleaner. He roamed all over Hindustan.

After a few years, when he went back to Rawalpindi, Lakhbeera visited his house. His father had expired. He met his stepmother and his brothers and sisters. His brothers had grown up, were studying in school, and the mother was running the shop.

They accepted him, but he was not cut out for domestic duties. Lakhbeera left again. Once again, he got off at the same station – Campbellpur.

The same dhaba owner took him in. He did not shirk hard work.

After all these years, he had himself become the owner of a dhaba. Trucks would come, halt here and leave. He did not marry. He did have a relationship with a woman or two, but it never worked. Next to his dhaba was a liquor joint. And in the shack, he sat with Fauji near the one-eyed window.

After the fire in his shack, he asked Fauji, 'Tell me, did someone set fire to it or did it start on its own?'

Fauji's eyes flashed for a moment and closed. Lakhbeera watched the eyeballs move behind his eyelids. Those eyes were thinking. There was something else on Fauji's mind.

Some days ago, Rai Bahadur Des Raj had sent for him. Des Raj was a well-known building contractor and got along well with the English. He wanted to send some of his domestic goods to Delhi. He had a good long-term working relationship with Ujagar Singh. Earlier too he had sent for something from Delhi. Or, maybe, something was sent to Delhi. Fauji didn't really remember. He got a good amount of money for the job – three hundred rupees, but now he was talking about a thousand.

'There is much more to carry, and the road has also become difficult. Earlier, one could go straight after getting on to G.T. Road. Now, they say people are attacked on that road frequently. The police stations are no longer functioning. Since the policemen have not been getting their salaries, they now participate in looting those travelling on G.T. Road. They snatch away whatever they can lay their hands on. One has to go through interior towns and districts to be safe.'

Before Fauji could think it over, Rai Bahadur explained the plan to him.

'Let me think about it,' said Fauji and left.

Since then, Fauji had been thinking of Rai Bahadur's offer. If that worked out, why not take Panna along with the goods? And Lakhbeera! Why not take him along too? Ever since Lakhbeera's shack had caught fire, he had started thinking. He felt that he should watch for a while. If the situation got worse, Rai Bahadur's family might come along as well.

Lakhbeera opened the second bottle and asked, 'Say, Fauji, if this fire did not start on its own, who could have set it off?'

Fauji responded philosophically, 'Are you asking for the name of the person or his religion?'

Fauji was not new to the city. Many people knew him in many ways. Ujagar Singh had brought him to the city. Though Ujagar hardly stayed in Campbellpur, his roots were here. He was born here and was brought up at his grandfather's farmhouse. His father, Dilawar Singh, had moved the family to Delhi when Ujagar was very young. He owned a taxi which operated for Imperial Hotel. As his children grew up, they moved to different places. He had three daughters, all married in distant parts of Hindustan, one in Orissa, another in Rajputana and the third in the United Provinces. Ujagar married a girl from the neighbourhood.

Ujagar continued to live with his parents along with his wife. In childhood whenever Ujagar visited his grandfather, accompanied by Dilawar, the grandfather would keep him back for a few days more, saying, 'Let him stay with me for some time. I will teach him Urdu. You're anyway becoming an angrez, replaced your pajamas with patloons. Take away your daughters, make mems of them and send them off to Englistan.' Then, he would add jovially, 'What's wrong with that anyway, eh?'

Ujagar liked to visit his grandfather even after he grew up. Dilawar did miss his father but never made it to Campbellpur again. Even after his grandfather's death, Ujagar would visit the farmhouse where he used to listen to tales of the British Raj. His grandfather admired the British.

His grandfather had always wanted Ujagar Singh to join the army and fight for the country. But Ujagar followed in his father's footsteps and expanded the business. Soon, they had three taxis. Around the time the third taxi arrived, Dilawar Singh passed away. Ujagar Singh brought his ashes to his grandfather at Campbellpur and scattered them over the fields as per his desire.

Sometimes, Ujagar thought of his grandfather's

words. There was no pattern to them – he said whatever came to his mind. 'Beta, it's like this – at least the British built a nation out of our country. Or else, we would have remained divided into little rajwadas, constantly fighting each other. They did not bring armies with them. They knew that our differences were as intense as our friendships. They created armies out of our own people and won our country. Really amazing, these English people! See? They got the rail started, established the postal system. And it's not as if they brought any money from their homes. The money was ours and so was the country, yet they became the masters and we, the servants.' He laughed and continued, 'Driving them away may not be a good idea. Once they leave, the differences will resurface.'

Soon, his grandfather too passed away. Ujagar Singh sold his land but retained his farmhouse.

After the taxis, he took to driving a bus from Campbellpur to Delhi, Delhi to Campbellpur. When he incurred losses with the bus service, he replaced it with two trucks. He did not abandon his roots in Campbellpur and would drive down often.

One rainy night, on his way to Campbellpur, Ujagar met with a serious accident on a bridge. An approaching truck crashed into his and left half of it dangling precariously off the bridge. The windscreen shattered into a spray of shards over Ujagar's face. Though the other truck driver was also injured, he had the presence of mind to use a rope and rescue Ujagar Singh. The instant he pulled Ujagar to safety, the truck plummeted into the river.

It was there, at the bridge and above the river, that Ujagar met Fauji. Fauji put him in his own truck and brought him to Campbellpur. He took Ujagar to his farmhouse and looked after him well, laying out a charpai for himself at Lakhbeera's dhaba.

After he had recovered, Ujagar Singh pooled his two trucks with Fauji's and they became business partners. When he offered his farmhouse for Fauji to stay in, the latter refused. He then got Fauji a place at the adda. It had an office-like space downstairs, and a living area upstairs, with an open terrace. He told him, 'You are the manager here and also my partner. You can run the business as you like. I'll keep visiting. I have another business in Delhi. With Waheguru's grace, the businesses will flourish.'

This was about four or five years ago, when the World War was at its peak and trucks used to be requisitioned at the cantonment. Everyone made money in the war. Petrol could be bought only with a permit. Fauji used to go to the cantonment and manage the permits. He was adept at paying off the officers, including the white ones. Fauji would say, 'They take bribes too, the goras, but not as blatantly. They never dirty their hands. They use knives and forks even to eat. With one hand they carve us up, with the other they devour us.'

Now, Fauji belonged to Campbellpur for all practical purposes.

He helped many a people of the city in dealing with the British, making payoffs wherever necessary. It is a different matter that people often greased his palm as well, but Fauji always respected the friendships he forged. He was a Pathan in such matters. He never went back on his word. And Lakhbeera was the closest of his friends; Fauji had even got him his liquor shop licence.

Since Lakhbeera's shack had caught fire, he had asked Fauji twice, 'Tell me, who do you think set the house on fire?'

Instead of answering, Fauji referred to the insignia Lakhbeera had painted on the dhaba's signboard. 'Aren't you afraid? You are a Sikh. You have got the khanda displayed so prominently.'

Lakhbeera's hand froze on its way to his lips.

That night, he lay in his bed, thinking. The fire in his tandoor had not yet gone out. He picked up a piece of burning wood and scraped the part of the board that had the khanda, blackening it ... He did not have the heart to scour it out.

At the adda, people had started calling Chandu 'dungar chor', the cattle hustler. Whenever he set out in a truck, he would pick up stray goats or cows and sell them to butchers. Soon, the truck drivers began mocking him, mooing and bleating when he approached the adda. 'Mind your goats, oye!' someone would call out.

One day, Chandu picked a fight with Fauji, who thrashed him so badly, he left the adda for good.

It was Chandu that Tiwari's wife was talking about that day.

'You know, your friend … that truck fellow…'

'Chandu?' Tiwari caught on at once.

'Yes, that's right … that dungar chor who keeps stealing other people's cattle…'

'What friend? I just happen to know him.'

'He does a lot of such things. Picking up a cow or goat from one place, selling it at another...'

Tiwari understood what she meant. 'Cattle is one thing, but to carry away a girl...' Suddenly, his voice fell to a whisper. 'There is a lot of difference between a butcher's shop and a brothel. The mute, after all, cannot protest, but her tongue works frantically like scissors.'

Kanta, the daughter-in-law, overheard their conversation. As it is, she lived in fear and now her blood ran cold. Somehow, she managed to disappear into the night with her son.

Tiwari and his wife searched high and low at every ashram and gurudwara, but found no trace of her. Fearing shame, they did not utter a word about it.

One day, Tiwari went looking for Chandu at the adda and came across Fauji.

'There's some stuff I want to send out,' Tiwari said.

Fauji asked him, 'What is it?'

'Some people will go. I may go myself.'

'In the truck?'

'There will be some baggage as well.'

'Where to?'

'Meerut.'

Fauji found it fishy and chanced his luck. 'Will get you to Delhi ... I'll take ten thousand. How many passengers?'

'Hmph!' said Tiwari, before he stormed away.

Once again, Fauji was filled with a strange foreboding.

Painti-Chhatti came up with another piece of explosive news.

'Do you know what's going on in your neighbourhood? All the Hindu men in Meeran village have been circumcised. All of them have turned Sunnis.'

No one wanted to believe this, but Painti-Chhatti put his hand over his heart and said, 'I swear. First, they got together and formed a peace committee. There were just a few Hindu households. Everyone was called to the masjid and told, "See, we don't want any violence here. We will protect you as best we can, but we are in the midst of madness. We are being pressured to mark houses belonging to Hindus. We have said that all Hindus have left. And those remaining have converted to Islam. Now, before they come for your lives, all you have to do is prove you are Musalman.'"

Pali asked, 'So?'

'So what? All agreed.'

'And the women? What proof will they have?' Pali asked.

Lakhbeera threw his shoe at him. 'Oye, you son of a bitch, enough! Don't you know where to stop? This is no joke. I hear a lot is happening on the other side too. The sardars have wreaked havoc!'

Painti-Chhatti said, 'They have done no less. In fact, we hear that they have massacred a train full of people and sent it to Lahore from Amritsar. Even the rail tracks are red with blood.'

A deep silence descended over the gathering. Painti-Chhatti said again, 'It's not really the neighbours who kill, it's their associates who do it. I have seen gangs of people wandering around. It's almost as if they have been specifically engaged for this ... to set fire, murder, loot. On top of this, they get money.'

'Who gives them money?'

'Those who receive what is looted. Committees have been set up. Wait and watch. These are the very people who will rule over us. These are the people who go from place to place spreading terror. They abduct women from the camps.'

'Camps?' a few chorused. 'What camps?'

Painti-Chhatti kept moving around restlessly, gathering news and rumours alike. There was not a single day he was not on the road between Campbellpur and Rawalpindi. G.T. Road was growing more dangerous by the day, so he used bypasses that went through villages, small towns and cities. Grain markets continued to function; in fact, they witnessed frenzied business. If he had a slow day, he would grow restless to take to the road. The turbulence all around made him anxious. In his travels, he witnessed things he could not come to terms with. This was an aspect of humanity he had ever expected to see.

The year '47 had dawned. The political climate was changing, and the situation on the ground was getting worse. As the date for Independence neared, freedom seemed more and more distant.

Here and there, military trucks were seen on the roads. People hoped that the army would help them cross the border. Those who had decided to leave began to gather together. Camps with barbed-wire fences were being set up for them.

Lakhbeera asked, 'But who is organizing food for them?'

'No one.'

Characteristically, Pritpal responded, 'So?'

'So, nothing! People from nearby villages distribute food and water. When one is hungry, caste, community and religion cease to matter. They are running from the very people who now feed them!'

Lakhbeera got up thoughtfully to attend to an errand inside. As he came out, he heard Hameed's loud voice booming, arguing about jhatka and halal. Pali must have said something. He had the habit of instigating people. But when Lakhbeera came out and joined them, Hameed fell silent. Pali turned away.

That night, as Pali lay asleep on a charpai outside his shack, Hameed chopped his head off with one blow of a cleaver. No one in the city saw him after that.

Fear gripped Campbellpur like never before. So far turbulent, the town came to a standstill. Fear crippled everyone. Disturbing news started to pour from the other side of the city as well.

The piece of meat had dislodged from Fauji's tooth. He advised Lakhbeera, 'You must go away for a few days.'

'Where?'

'The other side!'

'I have no one there. Everyone I know is here.'

Fauji said thoughtfully, 'God knows where Hameed has gone. Lock up your dhaba and liquor shop and come. I'll drop you off at Ujagar Singh's. This is going to get worse.'

Lakhbeera found this reasonable, but it made him think: What can Hindustan offer me? Why should I leave my country for another? If Pakistan, so be it – this is my country.

The next day, Rai Bahadur Des Raj asked Fauji, 'So, Faujdar, have you thought about ... when should we leave?'

Fauji had decided. 'Ji, let's leave the day after, on Jumma ... Friday.'

Lala Des Raj came closer and said, 'Of course, there's some baggage too, and I, along with my family, wish to leave this place. We'll return after things settle down...' He lowered his voice a little. 'The situation doesn't appear to be good at all ... and there is no question of going by bus or train. It's no longer one or two people, they are slaughtering trainloads. I don't feel confident travelling by car either. I can think of no other way.'

'How many are you?'

'There will be my wife, daughter, son and me.'

Fauji tried to be as gentle as he could. 'I know it may be difficult, but please don't bring too much luggage. I have three or four more people to take along.'

Rai Bahadur hesitated a little. 'Okay ... who else?'

Before Lala-ji could say anything else, Fauji said, 'They are leaving out of fear too. Look at the situation! I know some of them. And the truck belongs to Ujagar Singh. You know that. I'll hand it over to him and come back. We must leave the rest to Allah…'

Lakhbeera brought news that Tiwari had come.

'Really? What did he say?'

'He's ready to go to the other side. And he is also willing to give you the money you asked for.'

'I had only mentioned it in passing. He's Chandu's man.'

'He left an advance too. Here, look!' Lakhbeera showed him a bundle of notes and said, 'He's not short of money – he's a big wholesaler.'

Fauji placed his hands on Lakhbeera's shoulders gently. 'You haven't said anything so far. If you come, we will go. There are some other people too. Or else, I stay with you. And from today, you will stay at my place, not at the dhaba.'

Lakhbeera agreed. 'That incident with Pali left me … shaken. Let's go … It seems even my dhaba's days are numbered. We'll take a call when we come back!'

When he tried handing over the money, Fauji pushed it firmly into Lakhbeera's pocket.

'Keep it. There'll be more soon.'

That night, on the terrace, Fauji and Lakhbeera lay awake for a long time, watching the stars. Suddenly, Fauji asked, 'Beere, tell me, what is freedom? Where does it come from? For whom?'

These questions were too profound for Lakhbeera. At length, he said, 'The news about our departure has spread.'

'People have grown extra ears. They hear you even if you whisper into your pillow.'

Silence descended again. Fauji did not ask who had said what. At some point, they drifted into sleep. The sky above went its way, the earth below, its own.

The sun was yet to rise when the city woke up to a hushed hum. Many people made their way to the rooftops.

Muffled noises broke the silence. A long caravan of people walked along the city's roads. Bundles on their heads, boxes on shoulders, children in their arms and dragging the elderly along. These people were leaving their land. Overnight, they had been assigned a new country.

While those leaving were terrified into silence, those watching were choked with emotion. Only footfalls echoed in the silence of the night.

Fauji saw them and so did Lakhbeera as they looked down. Umar Sheikh and his family were also on the roof of their house. Master Karam Singh watched too, with his daughter-in-law and son, all still as statues.

Nobody called out to anyone. No eyes met. People kept mushrooming on terraces, watching in silent remorse. It was hard to believe the unfolding tableau. Was this the face of freedom? Did freedom entail such trauma?

Master Karam Singh's faith lay shattered. He spent the day chopping wood in the courtyard. Nobody stopped him. Neither Avtar Singh, nor his bahu. Both knew he was wrestling with himself. He only stopped to feed Bhuri. Once, he said to Avtar, 'No one has brought your bebe. Maybe all of this is going on there too.' Then he muttered to himself, 'Ever since the World War started ... Fazal used to say, doomsday is upon us. Now, I believe him.'

Restless, Karam Singh left the house for some time that day. When he returned, his face was pale and his lips were trembling. He called Bahu and said, 'The city is shrouded in a deathly silence ... wonder if it's the lull before the storm. Beta, carefully put aside whatever money and valuables we have. Everybody is gathering at Jajhar Gurudwara. Perhaps from there…' his voice choked as he said this, 'some kafila will start moving, like the one we saw today. Or if the military men come, trucks may be used to get people out. Only Waheguru knows what's in store!' His voice faltered. He went inside, picked up a khes, spread it over Bhuri and left with the buffalo.

Satya asked, 'Where are you headed?'

'I'll be back. Tell Avtar that Gyani-ji has asked everyone to gather at the chowk at dawn tomorrow. After the kirtan, we will all leave for the gurudwara.'

'But where are you going with Bhuri, Bhapa-ji?'

'We can't abandon this helpless creature, beta. I'll leave her with someone.'

The day grew darker; evening fell as if the heavens had thrown a net over the earth. The call of the azaan broke the silence. Once, this had been a calming sound. Master-ji would close his eyes and fold his hands. Now, he was gripped by fear. Earlier, he knew that the faithful were being called to worship in the masjid. Now, who knew why they were being summoned. The roads lay vacant. As he went through the bazaar, he saw some people sitting around the oven at Nanbai's bakery. Some people craned their necks to see where he was taking the buffalo.

Master-ji turned into a lane.

Within the lane, in another gali, was Master Fazal's house. Master-ji stood at the door for some time. His hand went up to knock, then fell to his side on its own. He tied the buffalo to the doorknob and left. After a while, when the buffalo moved, the door shook. Master Fazal opened the door and was surprised to see the animal. He lifted the khes and saw what was written on the animal's back with a chalk: 'I am sorry. I'm leaving Pakistan in your custody.'

In the morning, when Avtar Singh and his wife were ready to leave for the chowk, they discovered that Bhapa-ji was nowhere to be seen. They called out for him. Avtar said, 'Could he have gone to Umar Sheikh's place?'

'How is that possible? It was from his rooftop last night that there were calls of "Allah hu Akbar".'

Satya suddenly remembered. 'Oh, he has gone to fetch Beeji.'

That is why he had been asking about Phajju, the man with the bullock cart.

At the Ghantaghar Chowk, Sikhs and Hindus had already gathered, carrying their little trunks. Most people were carrying bundles. Kirtan had commenced. Women, men and children ... all were present. Their devotional chants spoke of unity, but their hearts pulsed with fear and anger. Their faces were clouded with sorrow. Five nihangs in saffron turbans stood in the front, holding naked swords. When the procession started moving towards the gurudwara, Avtar and his wife, carrying two small bundles, almost ran to join them.

At the same chowk, on the other side of the Ghantaghar, stood Fauji's truck. His passengers had arrived, carrying a huge amount of luggage including gold wall clocks, silver utensils and much more.

He explained to them patiently, 'Lala-ji, to carry this kind of baggage would mean inviting looters. People will not let us leave with all this. News has travelled ahead of us. Leave as poor travellers. Save your lives, that should be enough.'

Though he addressed Lala-ji, everyone present

got the message. Some boxes were opened. A few bundles were repacked. Whatever was left behind was arranged properly and, god knows why, covered with a sheet. Lala-ji got in with his wife and two children. They had placed two trunks there earlier. When Lala Des Raj saw Panna with a small trunk and a bundle, he avoided making eye contact and hoped that no one saw Panna's silent greeting. Only she had that special way of showing courtesy.

Seeing Kanta and Guddu, his grandson, Tiwari called Fauji aside and asked: 'How have the mother and child landed here? From where did they get so much money?'

Fauji asked him, 'Isn't she your bahu?'

He refused point-blank. 'No, ji. She is dead ... but this one...'

Fauji cleared the confusion: 'Umar Sheikh paid a good amount and said, help her cross the border and my Haj will be done. She is like my daughter, he said.'

Kanta and Guddu got on to the truck, somewhat frightened. Tiwari's wife had already found a place.

Tiwari asked, 'Shall I sit in front with you, Fauji?'

'No, my friend will sit there. Lakhbeera! Come now, climb up. Let's go … in the name of Allah.'

Winter was on its way out but the breeze still had a nip. The morning air was especially biting. Wrapped up in shawls and sheets, all of them resembled the bundles they were carrying. Only their heads peeped out. Their eyes were tearful. Some for leaving their motherland behind, others, perhaps, their valuables. It is not easy to leave behind one's roots. Not knowing when, where or if at all they would grow new ones. They had seen branches fallen from trees, withering away in the dust.

With each mile, the hope that they would ever return began to recede.

Still, Rai Bahadur asked his wife, 'Hope you didn't leave the keys of the kothi at the chowk?'

The wife shook her head. 'No, they are with me.'

It took the truck one-and-a-half hours to get out of the city. They saw no other truck on the way. A

71

horse rider came into view at a distance. And then a bullock cart appeared, rattling along on its way. There was a strange kind of loneliness. No one spoke.

Lakhbeera was uncharacteristically quiet too. He surveyed the surroundings wide-eyed. Once, he glanced through the small rectangular window at the back of the driver's cabin. There was no movement at the back. Both of Lala Des Raj's children were asleep. Nine or ten years of age, his daughter looked older; on the other hand, his older son looked just nine or ten! His spectacles had slipped down from his nose. Panna's eyes were closed but she was awake. Guddu lay sleeping in Kanta's lap and Kanta was looking at the sky. It was only Tiwari whose eyes were fixed on Kanta. His wife was now beginning to doze off.

Fauji stopped the truck at a crossing. Lala-ji sat up, alert. Lakhbeera looked around. Fauji made a decision. 'We'll go via Moosa Khail. If all goes well, we will get on to G.T. Road ahead.' The truck started to move again.

Rai Bahadur heard this, or gathered what was intended. He raised himself up on his knees, peeped through the window and said, 'Fauji, drive down the by-lanes to Miyanwali. It is better to go through small towns. There's more danger in big cities.'

Fauji nodded and Des Raj sat down again.

They had only journeyed an hour or two before the sun was directly overhead. Though its warmth was soothing, the light exposed them all. Villages around them too became visible.

This was when a minor incident occurred. The truck was lumbering ahead on an uneven road when they saw a small caravan of people at some distance across the fields. Their turbans and attire made it obvious that they were Hindus. All together they must have been about a hundred or so. Fauji parked the truck behind a few trees. Just then, a ten-year-old Sikh boy came running. He was holding the hand of an old man, perhaps his grandfather. Fauji stepped out of the truck. The boy raised his hand on seeing him and shouted, 'O bhai, are you going towards the border?'

This word 'border' had become rather common. Another word that was often heard these days was 'refugee'. As the boy came closer, he repeated his question, adding, 'Take my baba, he can't walk any farther.'

Fauji asked, 'And you? How will you go?'

Innocent desperation masked his face. 'If there's space, I'll come too.'

'And if not?'

'I will … with those people there…' He pointed to the caravan in the distance.

Fauji pulled down the plank at the back of the truck. 'Come along, beta … climb up.'

The boy said to Baba, who was barely able to stand with the help of a stick: 'Come, Baba … get into the truck.'

'And your father and mother? Where are they?' asked Fauji.

'They were both killed by those people. They'd have killed me as well but Dada hid me among the buffalo's fodder. And they did not do anything to Dada.' The boy said this mechanically, almost as if he were reading out an essay. There wasn't a trace of emotion in his voice.

Fauji did not ask any more questions. He helped them both into the truck.

Tiwari looked at Fauji sharply and muttered, 'They have had it very cheap!' Fauji pulled the plank back in place and climbed to his seat.

His passengers seemed to have brought along everything but food and water. Some said they had left it with the other things they had unloaded at the chowk. Others had completely forgotten about food. When Baba's grandson said, 'I'm thirsty, Masi-ji, is there water?', Tiwari looked at his wife, who replied, 'I had brought some … but it was in the silver surahi I left behind at the chowk.'

Des Raj's family looked at each other. Panna took out a small container from her bundle and offered it to the child. 'There is no glass, Kaka. Drink it straight from the container.'

Kaka raised his voice and asked, 'Baba, do you want to drink some water?' Baba nodded and, as was common practice, he drank without touching the rim of the container to his lips. A lot was drunk and as much spilled. But who was to say anything at that moment? After him, the grandson drank whatever little was left.

Guddu had woken up. He whispered to his

mother, 'I am hungry, Ma.' Kanta had brought thick gur-bajra rotis. Sheikh's wife had made them. She broke the rotis into pieces and handed one to her child, and also to the sardar kaka. She also extended some to Panna, who sat apart from the rest. The others had distanced themselves from her. Panna accepted a piece and expressed her gratitude by touching it to her forehead. Kanta took her to be a Musalman. But then why was she leaving? She could not ask now, but decided to do so later.

After a while, Lala Des Raj slid closer to the rear window of the driver's cabin. Peeping through it, he asked, 'Fauji, can we get something to eat and drink on the way? That was a blunder … to leave the basket of food at the chowk.'

Fauji replied, 'No doubt it's taking time, Lala-ji, but we are trying to stay clear of towns and cities.'

'No, no, you're right. That's how it should be.'

Lakhbeera said, 'Look to your right at the basti we've just left behind – you see the smoke? It's not from a mill or factory.'

Lala Des Raj turned. He could make out that some houses were burning. No matter how long it took on this road, it was without doubt a wise choice.

Over an hour later, a town loomed ahead.

Fauji asked, 'Shall we enter? There must be some shops open.'

Lakhbeera said in a whisper, 'Yes, go ahead. But keep the engine running. Just in case we have to make a run for it...'

By then Fauji had entered the town. Hasanabad. It wasn't a very big town and not very crowded either. But the tension in the air was palpable. Some shops were open. When the truck slowed down, some people turned to watch. Yet others came forward to peep inside.

'Where is the truck from? What are you carrying?' somebody shouted.

You couldn't tell from their faces and attire whether they were Hindus or Muslims. Before Fauji could decide on what to say, a person on a cycle grabbed the door of the truck.

'You look like a Muslim. Where are you going?'

Fauji replied sternly, 'Nowhere. It's none of your business.' He removed the man's hand from the door.

Untroubled, the man kept pedalling away alongside the truck. 'Really? So, shall we tell you where to go?'

Lala-ji sidled up to the window. 'Fauji, don't stop here. We don't want anything.'

Lakhbeera urged his friend on. 'Move fast, Fauji. This is not the right kind of place to stop.'

Hearing the ruckus created by the cyclist, a man on an approaching motorcycle raised a hand to stop the truck. A truck approached from the opposite side. Fauji turned into a lane. He could not speed up. They could have got stuck in a narrow lane. But when he heard the motorcycle still following, Fauji switched gears and sped through, mowing down crates and other objects – a charpai here, a couple of drums there – till he reached an outer road. Lakhbeera kept shouting, 'Left right, right left' as Fauji negotiated the truck. They could hear some trunks at the back sliding and falling, and the suppressed groans of the people who were being thrown this way and that. But till such time as the sound of the motorcycle ceased, Fauji did not let up.

After they had left the town well behind, Fauji

asked Lakhbeera: 'Shall we stop and check on the passengers sitting at the back?'

'Not here. We'll stop when we find a safe space.'

They had gone about fifteen miles when a station wagon with a wooden body, stuffed with passengers, overtook them and drove ahead. Rai Bahadur wished that he too had brought along his Buick. They would probably have made it faster and carried some more luggage too. But who knows. He sighed.

Two miles further up, off the road, a bungalow came into view. It could have belonged to a wealthy family, but had clearly been ransacked. Fire had blackened its walls, windows and doors.

Fauji looked at Lakhbeera, who was gaping at the sight. He said, 'Seems to have been abandoned.'

'Someone must live there,' Lakhbeera reasoned.

'Doesn't look like it. But it is secluded. We may find a water tap there. There may just be a well.'

Fauji turned the truck in that direction.

They stopped outside the gate and parked the truck, its front facing the road. Just in case. Lakhbeera said,

'If there had been anyone in there, the sound of the truck should have drawn them out. You stay at the wheel … I'll have a look.'

Fauji also got down from the truck. 'You'll not go alone,' he said.

They were in the compound when a Pathan appeared. He held a lathi with brass fittings at one end.

'Oye! Who's there, oye?' It seemed he had been expecting someone else. 'Who is it?'

'Khan sa'ab, we need water. We have people travelling with us. They are thirsty.'

The Pathan noticed the truck, seemingly for the first time. It was stationed outside. Suddenly, his voice toughened.

'What have you come for? On what business? May Allah smite you hard! Get out, get out of here!'

Khan's voice was edged with anger and fear. His face had turned red. He could have used his lathi, but Fauji's manner seemed to deter him.

'We are not rioters, Khan. Allah-qasam, we are all desperate refugees. There are women … we have children with us. We only—'

Suddenly, there were sounds from inside. Somebody was locked within. Upon being asked, the Pathan revealed that the house belonged to one Kavishwar Singh. Rioters had tried to burn it down. A few days back, they left two women locked inside a room.

'They do bad things to them. Beat them and then tie them up. They keep coming and threaten to kill me.'

'So, what are you doing here?'

'Oye, sardar sahib has kept me as a chowkidar. When he comes back, how will I explain this?'

So, it was duty that kept the naïve Pathan there. He seemed to have no idea that the nation was being torn into two, that freedom was coming and that Kavishwar Singh might never return.

Fauji tried to explain the situation to him. He tried very hard. Lakhbeera pulled out a bundle of notes and pushed it into Khan's pocket. 'Khan, for Allah's sake, save your life. Take this money and go back to Kabul … where are you from?'

Khan stared at him wide-eyed and then, suddenly, took Fauji's hand and said, 'Oye, listen. You too are a Musalman. Do something good before you go. Take these two women with you. There, anywhere. Those people ... Those sons of bastards will come again, rape them, sell them or kill them...'

Before he could say anything more, Fauji held his hand and went to the room where the two women were locked up. They were sisters it seemed. They resembled each other and were around the same age.

The two women did not stop trembling until they boarded the truck.

Tiwari raised his eyebrows. 'You demanded a lot of money from us, Fauji, and now you are picking up passengers at random! What will you do with them?'

Fauji clenched his teeth. He would have exploded but controlled himself. No one said another word to him.

The truck lurched into motion. The sisters sat huddled together. One of them began to chant the Gurbani under her breath. Both had an iron bangle on their arms. They were probably Sikhs.

Once they had driven some distance, the people

in the truck realized that, in all the confusion, they had forgotten to pick up water.

It had been nearly half a day since Fauji had left the chowk.

It had been half a day for those who had started from the chowk for the gurudwara, reciting prayers for peace. All of them had reached the gurudwara, including Avtar and Satya. They were worried about Master-ji, less so about Beeji. She was, after all, with the family at Dera.

Master Karam Singh had woken up well before dawn that day – if he had slept at all.

He had taken out his old brown canvas shoes and kept them under his mattress. They were very old. From the time he used to take PT class at school. The shoes fit tighter now. He had woken up at three in the morning and put them on. For a while, he lay in bed with his shoes on.

Assured by the gentle snoring of Avtar and his wife that they wouldn't wake up, he crept out of the house. He took the name of Waheguru as he slid open the latch of the door, closing it softly behind him. He then tiptoed across the lane. Once out of his area, he broke into a run. He was supposed to meet Phajju at Ganja Talao.

The Talao was an hour away. He began to pant much before he had anticipated. He had not factored in his age. Fortunately, he had left home early. Phajju had warned him, 'Bhapa-ji, the situation is not good. If I come into the lane, the sound of the cartwheels will wake up everyone.'

Karam Singh had not informed the children that he was going to fetch his wife. If he had told them, would they have allowed it?

Master-ji finally made it to the Talao and slumped under the age-old banyan tree, exhausted. Phajju had to call for him.

When they started, the sound of the cart seemed very loud. They were scared that the sun would wake up. They were out of Campbellpur when the sun rose, and their hearts began to thud. They passed a village. Then another. In the next, they saw some people going towards the village after their fajr-namaz. Dera was still quite a distance away. Some young boys came forward and stopped the cart.

'Hey, where are you taking the sardar?'

Karam Singh stood up. He pushed his kirpan under his kurta to hide it. Phajju hurled two abuses at them and pulled out his sword from under a sack. He swung his naked sword in the air and urged his oxen forward. The startled boys darted out of their way. The boys were probably unarmed. No one followed Phajju and Master-ji.

Phajju brought the cart to Dera and stopped it right in front of Nihal Singh's house. The house was in a lane open from both ends. As soon as Master-ji stepped down, Phajju advised, 'Bhapa-ji, don't take Bibi back immediately. Stay with your in-laws for a few days. It's dangerous.' He left without waiting for an answer.

Master-ji knocked at the door. It opened after a long while. Ghulam answered it and Tiger rushed out, barking. As soon as he saw Master-ji, Ghulam ushered him in and locked the door behind them. The house seemed vacant.

Master-ji learnt that his wife Harnam Kaur had left for the border with her daughter's in-laws. He was thunderstruck.

'How did they go?' He sounded flustered.

'A special train for refugees was leaving from Dera Jamali. The local zamindar escorted them to the station. They told me to inform you, but under the circumstances, how could I have done that?'

Just then, Hariram came out. Master-ji was surprised to see him. 'Didn't you go as well?'

Hariram was an old family servant. He was wearing a withered Turkish cap. His eyes grew tearful.

Ghulam said, 'He refused to leave Tiger behind.' Tiger was his pet dog.

Hariram said, 'How could I have left him here, Bhapa-ji? He was a tiny pup when he came and I...' He could not complete his sentence. Tears began to flow from his eyes.

'And if somebody sees you now?'

He quickly removed his cap and showed him his head.

'I have cut my choti – and Ghulam has given me this cap.'

'You mean, for this dog...'

'What "dog", Sardar-ji? I brought him up like my son. If they say, I shall become a Musalman, but I will not abandon him.'

Tiger, his tongue lolling, came and sat next to Hariram. Karam Singh patted his head gently.

But he was in a spot now. How was he to go back? It occurred to him that he could borrow a horse from the zamindar, but how would he return it? Karam Singh spent the day trying to think of a way out.

Lying in bed at night, Karam Singh grew restless. Finally, he did what he had done back home. After half the night had passed, he tiptoed out of the door and headed back towards Campbellpur. In the light of the half-moon, he could see a narrow path running through the fields; he followed it and eventually reached the road. But then he lost his way at some point and realized it only when he encountered a couple of pahalwans returning from their duty as guards at the masjid.

This was just outside Bundyala village. This was a village mainly of Muslims, and seeing a Sikh under suspicious circumstances, they immediately became violent. Their eyes were bloodshot. Karam Singh tried to think up a convincing story, but that made it worse. The pahalwans pulled out their axe and sword.

They took off his turban and tied it like a noose around his neck. Just then, a tall, tough-looking man emerged from the back and stopped them.

'Oye, hold on! That's my prey. I know this fellow.'

'Who is he?'

'He's one of those old Khalsa rebels from Campbellpur. I need to settle an old score with him. Chhadh de.'

He too had a large axe in his hands. Swiftly, he took hold of the turban and pulled Master-ji on to another path.

'Come here, Sardara! I have an old score to settle with you.'

His friends cautioned him, 'Be careful. We've taken away his kirpan, all right.'

They showed him the kirpan and moved on towards the village. The tall chap kicked Karam Singh with his heel and said: 'Come on, move!'

'Wh-where…?'

'Move, I said! There is a butcher's basti at the end of the village.'

They made their way to the basti. He pushed Karam Singh into a house and quickly closed the door behind him. His wife came out. No sooner had she screamed, the father rushed out.

'Oye, Baqar! What's this? Who is he?'

Karam Singh's loose hair partly revealed his face. Baqar handed him the turban and said, 'The guards were going to kill him. I caught hold of him and brought him here.'

Master-ji pulled aside his hair as he recognized Baqar's father. He was still standing in the courtyard. His eyes filled up with tears and his throat choked. 'Hashmat?' Master-ji whispered the name.

Holding him by the hand, Hashmat brought him into the room.

Hashmat was a butcher by profession. At one time, he wanted his son, Baqar, to be educated. He had gone to admit him in a school. Some bigots raised objections due to his religion and status. Master-ji had fought with many to get Baqar his admission. The next year, the issue was brought up again. Karam Singh was adamant. Master Fazal had done all he could to help Karam, but Rai Bahadur Des Raj had bribed an English officer to expel the boy. Even after the incident, Master Karam Singh taught Baqar at his home for a year. Finally, the boy abandoned his studies to participate in local dangals.

Karam Singh was keen to reach Campbellpur as soon as he could. Avtar and Satya might still be in the gurudwara. The caravan may not have left so early. But Hashmat would not allow that. He told Karam Singh how news spread in their small village. In fact, someone had even come to their door enquiring about Baqar. Hashmat had told him that he hadn't returned after his night watch yet. After Master-ji had had his bath, Hashmat persuaded him to dress up in the style of his own community of butchers, tying a tehmad around his waist. He told Karam Singh to keep his beard open. But what about the hair? Neither of them dared to address that.

In the afternoon, there was another incident. On a road a little farther from Bundyala, the one that stretched towards G.T. Road, a long convoy of military trucks passed by. Hindus and Sikhs were leaving the country. People climbed to their rooftops to see this. Master-ji wanted to see too. When he persisted, Hashmat convinced him to wear a Pathani fur cap.

A whisper coursed through the entire village. 'Hindus and Sikhs have left...' A lot of people choked up. Many were in tears. Something had come apart, leaving behind an emptiness.

The caravan of military trucks with refugees turned towards G.T. Road. It was at this point that Fauji had told Lakhbeera: 'We'll go via Moosa Khail. If all goes well, we'll get on to G.T. Road ahead.'

But he did not turn towards G.T. Road. After passing through the city of Khorda, and leaving behind Kavishwar Singh's kothi, the road was uneven, but there was no immediate danger. However, there was one minor irritant: the old Sikh Baba had urinated in his pyjamas. Kaka was terribly embarrassed.

'Now, what have you done, Babbe!' He did not know what to say. He took off Babbe's turban and started to wipe the floor with it. What else could he have done? Baba's mouth was half-open and he was sleeping. People had covered their noses. But Panna gently patted Kaka's head and made him sit beside her. She gathered the damp turban and threw it out. She said in rustic Punjabi, 'Sutt de, Kaka. Throw it away, we'll get another.'

When Des Raj conveyed the news, Fauji eased the truck to the side of the road. He got off and walked to the back of the truck. Lowering the plank, he announced, 'Anyone wanting to shit or pee may do so now.'

As far as the eye could see, there were jagged fields and uneven roads. A patchy forest lay in the distance. Some of Fauji's passengers stepped off.

Tiwari asked, 'What time do you think we'll reach?'

'Where?'

'I mean ... where are we going?'

'Don't you know?' Fauji's voice had an edge.

'I want to go to Dilli. That's what I paid you for.'

'You and your damn money! There's no way I'm going to Dilli. I'll drop you off whenever everyone feels we're at the border and safe. I have no idea where this border is and what it's called. If you know, tell me.'

Fauji moved away behind the bushes to relieve himself.

Hardly half an hour had passed since they were back on the road when Fauji stopped the truck. The passengers looked at each other, questions writ large on their faces. Lakhbeera turned towards him, then to the direction Fauji was looking in. At some distance, in the middle of the road, a station wagon stood, blocking the way.

'I don't see anyone around,' said Fauji.

'It's the same one.'

'Same what?'

'The one that overtook us this morning.'

'Were there any passengers in it?'

'It was full. There was a Sikh family. I saw women and children too.'

'Well, no one's here now.' Fauji paused before adding, 'Is it possible they have been looted?'

'What if the car broke down and the passengers abandoned it?'

Without further speculation, Fauji drove slowly towards the station wagon. Just then he spotted them: two sardars. They emerged from behind, guns in their hands. They wore what looked like army uniforms but without badges of any kind.

Fauji stopped. Now, he could see the whole family in the wagon.

One sardar came forward. 'We're out of fuel. Do you have petrol?'

Fauji stepped out of the truck. Lakhbeera hurried to his side.

'No,' said Lakhbeera.

The other sardar spoke. 'In that case, we'll take whatever is in your tank. If you create trouble, we will break open the fuel tank and take whatever we can.'

Fauji and Lakhbeera looked at each other. Lakhbeera said, 'We have a canister. Five gallons. You can take half.' He pulled out the canister from underneath the truck. Without uttering a word, one of the sardars took it away and walked towards his car. The other one stood before them, his gun ready.

The sardar emptied the canister into the station

wagon's tank. He started the car, flung away the empty canister, and called out to the second one, 'Come along, Balliya!'

That was when Lakhbeera caught hold of Billu.

'You bastard, let's see you get away now. The whole canister…'

Billu pushed Lakhbeera and ran. Lakhbeera recovered and got to his feet. The sardar in the car shot at him. The other one fired at Fauji but missed. Another bullet hit Lakhbeera and he fell. The bullet had passed through his heart.

None of the passengers in the truck moved. Everyone held their breath. The station wagon vanished from sight.

Fauji dropped to his knees. Lakhbeera was dead. Fauji sobbed, beat his head and started hurling abuses in desperation. God knows who he abused and to what end. One by one, everyone stepped off the truck.

It took Fauji an hour to compose himself. He had begun this journey only for his friend. If he had an option, he would have thrown away his keys, abandoned the truck and walked away. But there were women and children depending on him. Lakhbeera's bedding lay on top of the truck above the driver's seat. There was a small can of petrol too. Fauji threw them all to the ground.

He wrapped the body in the bedding and began collecting wood. Des Raj suggested the corpse be buried, else it would take a long time. The sun was already on the descent. Fauji refused. 'He was a Sikh … my friend. I will cremate him. Anyone in a hurry is free to leave.'

Tiwari stood up.

'Leave? How can we leave? We've already paid you. You are not taking us free of charge.'

A thought crossed Fauji's mind. Lakhbeera had put the cash in the pillow cover and wrapped the cover into the bedding. He pulled out the cover and tossed a fistful of notes in Tiwari's direction.

'Take your money. Take more than what you paid. I will not take you along.' He flung the pillow cover at him.

Lala-ji's son had fetched a bundle of logs. He seemed to have grown up suddenly. He placed them on the improvised pyre. Fauji picked up the tin of petrol and poured almost all of its contents on the corpse and the wood.

Des Raj said, 'Don't waste all of it...'

The look in Fauji's eyes silenced him.

Fauji lit the pyre. Bending down on his knees and with both hands raised, he read out the fateha. Wiping his eyes, he turned towards his truck. Everyone climbed in. He told Panna, 'You come here, in front. Sit with me.'

Fauji started to raise the plank of the truck to close it. Tiwari approached the truck. Fauji shoved him away. 'No. Go die in the wilderness.'

Fauji shut the plank.

'O, Fauji. My wife is in the truck. You keep all this...'

When he held out the money, Fauji kicked the whole bundle into the pyre. He asked Tiwari's wife, 'Do you want to die with him?'

The pale, frightened woman said nothing, but she shook her hand: no, no. She sobbed but shrank back into a corner of the truck.

Fauji climbed back into the driver's seat. Tiwari shouted at him, but Fauji paid no heed. He left with the rest of the passengers. Tiwari stood there, staring at the burning pyre.

The truck had come a long way. The silence between Fauji and Panna had broken. Panna must have asked something and Fauji was saying, 'My mother was the mistress of the nawab of Jaunpur. She used to sing. She sang very well, like you!' The sun was growing dim. Clouds hung about like wet nappies. They were in a hilly region now. As the truck lumbered on with some effort, Fauji continued, 'Once it so happened, she became pregnant. The nawab wanted the baby aborted. Amma ran away to Rawalpindi with her accompanist, the rabaab player.'

'Why Rawalpindi? Was it her home town?' Panna asked.

'No ... she hailed from somewhere on the same side. But Rawalpindi was a safe distance away from Jaunpur and her rabaabiya had close relatives there, I think.'

Panna looked at him searchingly, as if trying to read some emotion on his face. But no shadow marred his impassive countenance. He continued, 'A good fellow, the rabaabiya was. He used to say, "Except for the rabaab, I never learnt anything. What could I do? I had to bring you up. I was not prepared to join any kotha. For some time, I made a living running a tonga. It was hard. After the luxuries of the durbar, your mother could not cope with poverty. She went back to Jaunpur. I didn't. What could I have done? How could I have fed you? You learnt the ways of the world on your own. Life teaches you."'

Fauji fell silent again.

Panna said in a low voice, 'I am a mere wandering mirasi, but you are a nawabzada.'

When Fauji turned to look at her, Panna added: 'Yes … really … the son of a nawab.'

Fauji muttered, 'Yes, the bastard of a nawab.'

Lala Des Raj peeped through the window frame at the back of the cabin and said, 'Miyanwali is not too far now, Fauji. Once we reach there, then … then Poonch … and then Jammu!'

The truck had managed quite a distance uphill but there was still some way to go. It kept climbing at a steady pace, jerking and rickety. The sun was sliding down. A strange hum sounded in the distance. They stopped the truck to see what it was. Far below them, a caravan of refugees was passing by. It seemed small from the distance, but was enough of an indication for everyone that Fauji was on the right track.

The sky was turning red. Another few miles and they could begin their descent. As soon as the truck reached the top, one of the front tyres deflated.

'We'll have to stop for a while,' Fauji declared.

It looked like it would rain soon. Something like a ruin stood some distance away. Fauji said, 'Get down. It'll take me a while to change the tyre. See if you can get to…' His words trailed off as he picked up Guddu, carrying him off the truck.

Broken liquor bottles littered the ruin. Looters! God bless them, they had left behind a matka of water.

The darkness grew thicker. It began to drizzle. As he retrieved the spare, he felt a pang for Lakhbeera. He thought of Campbellpur, of the one-eyed window. Who remained in Campbellpur now? Everyone had left.

He found it hard to believe that Campbellpur would have no Sikhs, no Hindus. No Pali. No Lakhbeera.

Master Karam Singh was one of the few trying to return to Campbellpur. The day was drawing to a close here too. And nowadays the descending night felt like a shroud spreading over everyone.

Hashmat had convinced him to stay for the day. He had promised Karam Singh that he would get him to Campbellpur. As night approached, Master-ji's restlessness grew. He had suffered the last two nights the same way. His eyes were dry now. They were burning. But he could not sleep.

Hashmat got up at midnight and readied his horse. Despite Baqar's insistence, he had decided to do this himself. As a precaution, he gave Master-ji his salwar-kameez, wrapped him in a khes and placed a cap on his head.

It was the last quarter of the night when the horse galloped out of the village. There were guards on patrol near the masjid. One of them was Baqar.

Hashmat left Karam Singh off at the Campbellpur Ghantaghar Chowk, offering to accompany him up to the gurudwara. Master-ji refused and made him go back. He feared for his saviour's life. Karam Singh hurried to the gurudwara on foot, and was shocked to see that only two granthis remained there. The rest had left.

He did not stay either. He thought of going to Fazal's, but found himself in front of his own lane as he walked in a daze. It was quiet. He met no one. Campbellpur seemed to have become a ghost town. He stood at the front door. The latch was open, the way his children had left it. He entered, closing the door behind him. In the courtyard, Bhuri's place lay vacant. He sat in the courtyard for a long time, overcome by sleep.

Shaking himself awake, he entered the bedroom, and held his breath. His wife, her eyes wide open, lay on the bed. Lifeless. A blue froth oozed from her mouth, drying on the pillow. He clutched at his chest, frozen. He could not bring himself to touch her. Not even to close her eyes. He felt a strange contentment. It was all over.

When the sky shed its darkness, he got up. He collected the pieces of wood. It had taken days to cut them. He prepared the pyre. From the kitchen, he fetched tins of pure ghee and emptied them over the logs.

He went inside and covered his wife's body. Her cracked feet spoke of how far she must have run on roads strewn with dust and pebbles. Blood streaked her heels. He cleaned them. He brought the body out and lay it on the wood. He lit the fire and sat there, resting his head against the pyre.

The sky shed its dark attire and draped itself in morning light. The sun woke them up.

Resting against the wall, Fauji had fallen asleep. He blinked, got up and went to the rooftop to find Panna sitting there, her head wrapped in a dupatta. She moved a little when he sat down beside her.

He looked around the ruin. Two of the truck's tyres were flat now. It looked as though the truck were sitting on its knees. The stepney was lying at a distance. Some baggage was scattered around it.

He asked Panna, 'When did they all leave?'

'Last night … a caravan was passing by down below, carrying torches. One by one everybody went along. They gave up on the truck.'

Fauji said, 'I was half-asleep, didn't bother to stop anyone.'

He stood up and walked to the other end of the roof. Without turning back, he called out, 'Panna, come here...'

He looked over to his right. A huge caravan was going the other way. Limping and crawling. On carts, on foot, with bundles on their heads. They seemed to be worse off than what they had seen so far.

'They are going to Pakistan,' Fauji said.

'Where is that?' asked Panna.

Fauji had no answer. 'It will be somewhere. Someday.'

They stood on the rooftop for a long time, watching the never-ending caravan. Then slowly, they returned to where they had been sitting.

Fauji said, 'Panna, I can't take you to the border. This truck will have to be abandoned now.'

'And you? Where will you go?' she asked.

Just then, Kaka came running from the truck.

'O bhai, maiyya, Baba is dead!' he said, panting. 'My Baba is dead. What do I do?'

Panna called out, 'Come up, Kaka!'

Small batches of refugees were still passing by from the left of the mountain.

When Kaka came up, Panna rose to her feet and hugged him. 'Beta … you come along with me!' She had made her decision and said to Fauji, 'We'll go now.' She explained to Kaka that Fauji would perform the last rites for Baba. 'There's no need to remain here any longer, beta.'

After Panna left with Kaka, Fauji walked out of the ruin all alone, leaving behind Baba's body. He walked slowly, turning right of the mountain, from where a long caravan moved towards an unknown destination.

PART TWO

Freedom arrived all right, but it came drenched in blood, wounded … the body slashed in different places. Some limbs were amputated, some left hanging, deformed, scarred.

As Master Fazal used to say, 'Millions will be crushed under the feet of this conceited history. The wounds will take decades to heal, centuries to overcome the trauma.'

The partition was supposed to happen over Bapu's body. And so it did. He was the first to go, felled by bullets – his killer a Hindu like him. He was India's Rashtra Pitah – Father of the Nation. Muhammad Ali Jinnah followed soon after. Pakistan's Qaid-e-Azam – Father of the Nation. Both countries lost their father's refuge.

Master Fazal had also said that a few names would stick to the fabric of time. And so they did. Pakistan's first prime minister Liaquat Ali was shot dead by his own countryman. Time took his name into safekeeping. A few years later, India's prime minister Jawaharlal Nehru passed away. Time engraved his name too.

The decades began rolling down. Raids across the border became commonplace. At times by tribes in military fatigues, at others by army men dressed as tribes.

If Master Fazal were alive, he would have said that the boys had started going to school. Breaking each other's slate, spilling inkpots, jabbing each other with pen nibs.

Refugee caravans gathered at camps, then began to spread out like pathways emerging from a jungle. People began to stoke their kitchen fires with whatever wood they could lay their hands on – damp or dry. Smoke filled the air. Famine, unemployment and hopelessness scaled new highs. History had seldom witnessed lost souls on such a scale.

The refugees who had started out with Fauji began

to disperse once they crossed over to Hindustan. They went in all directions. Someone knew a village. Another was aware of some city. Thousands started marching along rail tracks, hoping for some train to turn up or maybe a station which would provide them some direction. Refugee camps began sprouting all over. Mandirs and gurudwaras overflowed with sharanarthis. A new term was coined in place of refugees: 'sharanarthis'. Fauji's musafirs were all lost, like a few grains in a bounty of crops.

Kanta had travelled well past Attari with Guddu. A knowledgeable soul said, 'We've reached Amritsar – this must be the border.'

Tiwari's wife Damayanti had vomited a number of times on the way. She was running a high fever. After Tiwari had been left behind, she would not let go of her daughter-in-law. Stumbling, falling, she stuck around with Kanta. Many people fell by the wayside, injured, knocked down by high fever. No one stopped to enquire. Many died but no one stopped to mourn. God knows how Damayanti kept dragging herself along. Before she reached Amritsar, she suffered a severe bout of stomach ache and doubled over in pain under a tree. Kanta stopped for a moment, wondering if Damayanti had fainted. She put Guddu down, and after a minute or two started walking again, joining the weary caravan on its way.

Kanta took refuge in Gurudwara Harmandir Sahib, Amritsar. The langar there offered food twice a day. It was quite astounding how so much daal-roti and so many volunteers kept turning up under such circumstances. The crowd kept swelling. Kanta tied one end of her dupatta to Guddu's waist. The fear of losing him in the horde never left her.

One day, at the langar, Guddu's eyes fell on a man who seemed to be searching for someone frantically. He looked like he had lost his mind. His beard was overgrown, hair unkempt. Guddu thought that he looked rather familiar. When he pointed out the man to Kanta, she gasped. She immediately covered her son's face with her dupatta.

It was her father-in-law. Tiwari. How had he managed to reach here? Without wasting a moment, Kanta left not only the gurudwara but the camp itself.

Kanta was extremely distressed. Her parents were

in Delhi. She had been trying to get across some news to them for days, but to no avail. Post offices were closed. Telephone lines were down. All exchanges had failed. Everyone advised her to go to the CTO, Amritsar. Keep trying, they said. Only the radio was operational. Names and addresses of refugees were announced on it from six in the morning to ten at night. A volunteer of the Hindu Mahasabha had promised to broadcast her whereabouts on it. But he could not say when her turn would come.

Kanta could never overcome the fear of being seen by Tiwari. He could snatch the boy away. Wandering around the streets, she came to a road that people said connected Amritsar to Delhi. Kanta started walking on that road. It would reach Delhi someday. Even if it took months. She wasn't alone on that road either. Thousands kept marching on it day and night.

Soni and Moni had crossed the border and reached Amritsar to find the entire city turned into a large refugee camp. Besides the government-run camps, small groups of tents kept cropping up wherever they found space. Leave aside the border of the country, it was difficult to make out the city's boundaries. No one knew where they were. Men and women, young and old, drifted from one camp to another like dry leaves scattered by the wind.

There were many who had managed to reach Hindustan with their families intact, but lost each other in the chaos here. They were too bewildered to realize which way they were going. Those who had brought their wealth along were trying to shake off their relatives. Some were looking for cities they had read about, heard about or corresponded with. On the way, if they made friends, they would tag along.

There was no one with Soni and Moni. Their real names were Surjit and Manjit and they were probably twins. Both wore kadas on their arms. They were now separated from the group that had brought them to Amritsar. Familiar with Gurudwara Darbar Sahib, they went there and offered prayers, took a dip in the Sarovar and ate at the langar. They hid a roti each in their kurtis. Who knew if food would be available in the evening. Volunteers were distributing clothes, sheets and blankets to the needy. Soni and Moni got dupattas to cover their heads.

Life in a camp was not easy for two abandoned young women. All sorts of things were happening in the name of Waheguru. A volunteer even took them to the burnt-down house of a Musalman in some secluded lane. He tried to tempt them. 'People are grabbing up houses. We've saved this one. You can take the two rooms on the top floor, our family will stay downstairs.'

Soni-Moni fled in fear. The house looked like the one on the other side – where they had been locked up. If it weren't for the truck driver … would they still be alive? Who knows?

After that episode, the sisters became cautious. But what could they have done when horde after horde kept arriving? With every new horde, the one that had come earlier kept getting pushed out. It was impossible to stay on.

From Amritsar, trains set out in different directions. Buses too. There were trucks as well, but only for those who could afford them. There were no tickets you could buy, so the trains ran as they wished. People got on whatever train left earlier. Everyone was desperate to leave this city of camps. Get out one way or another.

After they had been pushed around for weeks, Soni and Moni too got on one such train. They didn't know where the train disgorged them. Some passengers said, 'Not here … change the train … we have to go further.'

They spent some days on that platform and then boarded another train. They kept criss-crossing cities the way trains change tracks. Even after reaching Hindustan, they could not find a place to settle down. Days stretched to months.

Moni grew sickly. Her face turned pale. Soon, she began throwing up. That was when she realized she was carrying the child of her rapist. There was no way she could abort the pregnancy. No opportunity. The passage seemed endless.

Moni would beat her belly and cry, 'This is my enemy growing in my belly. What should I do? It will die only if I die!'

People started sticking together. They moved in groups. There was another kind of group, of thugs, who were taking advantage of the refugees. Some volunteers would fill up a bus to take refugees from railway stations to camps. Halfway through, they would ask for the fare, threatening to drop them off in the middle of nowhere. Who wants to get off alone on a deserted road? One person would take something out of a secret pocket, another would take off a bangle or two. Sometimes, someone would help his fellow traveller. The homeless have tremendous compassion. But they were muhajirs even in their own land. They were sharanarthis.

The refugees had set up home in Bundi fort. Volunteers from the Rashtriya Swayamsevak Sangh were helping everyone. After nine hundred years, a saffron flag flew over the fort. It is here that the matriarch of a Punjabi family, Bebe, recognized Moni's condition. Her belly betrayed her pregnancy.

There was no man with them. When Bebe enquired, Soni lied, 'Our family, including Moni's husband, was killed on the other side. Moni was with child. We fled. We got on a truck full of refugees.'

Bebe had nine sons. All of them had managed to escape with their families. They had been able to bring along a lot of their wealth, although all their property, cattle and some other possessions were left behind. Only the grandfather had stayed back. Until the very end, he kept repeating, 'You will all come back. Wait and see. Allah willing, this calamity too will blow over...' He used to take the name of Allah in the same breath as he uttered Waheguru.

Bebe wandered around the fort with a chhadi. The sons sometimes joked, 'Bebe, in an earlier life, you must have been a maharani here. Was this your fort?'

She'd pull her dupatta over her head and say, 'Of course. And these are all my subjects!'

Bebe was very much like a maharani.

One day, she landed up at the turret in a corner of the fort's terrace where Soni and Moni had set up their dwelling.

'How are you, girls? I see you both going down every day.' There was a basti below, close to the river.

'We go to the village there, Beeji, looking for work.'

Moni picked up a canister and got up to leave. Soni continued to talk.

'What kind of work?' Bebe asked.

'Anything. From washing clothes to washing utensils ... whatever work...'

'Do you get paid?'

'They are not rich people, Beeji. They don't need servants. Just a little helping mud plastering or ... They give us what they can.'

'Where are you from?'

'Khorda, Zila Campbellpur. And you?'

'From Dera Khail Khan ... not very far from Attock. You know, Campbellpur used to be called Attock.'

Meanwhile, Moni had returned, her canister filled with water. Her back hurt when she bent to set it down.

Bebe asked, 'Have you sprained your back? Come here, beti. I'll rub it. Don't lift heavy things.'

Then she looked at Soni and said, 'I have been watching her for days. I know she is with child. That's why I came over to ask about her. Is there no one else with you?'

Neither of the sisters answered. Moni's already sallow complexion became paler and Bebe understood it all.

'Nine sons have I produced, beti. I know each and every aspect of motherhood. I longed to have a daughter, but Waheguru willed otherwise.'

Soni said in a whisper, 'Do you have your sons with you? All of them?'

'Three of them are with me. Two left earlier. About twelve or fourteen miles away, in Kota, there's a village. Called Alpha. Named by an Englishman. They have gone to see the land. Back there, we were farmers.'

Stroking Moni's belly, she asked, 'Where's the father?'

Moni choked back her tears.

Soni lied, 'Killed in Khorda. All were killed. We were saved by ... a truck driver who ... who was escorting refugees...'

Leaning against her stick, Bebe climbed down the turret and disappeared into the fort.

In the late afternoon, she came back. She said to Moni, 'Look here, dear. If there's life in the womb, you are still a suhagan. Wear this black thread on your neck. Think of it as auspicious. You are still married and not a widow.' She left, transforming an unmarried girl into a married one.

A strange game of hide-and-seek began between Bebe and Moni. When she left the turret, Moni would check if Bebe was around. As for Bebe, whenever she emerged from the veranda across, her eyes rose up to the turret. Whenever Bebe met Moni, she offered some pregnancy-related advice. She'd tell her about home remedies, give her some recipes and ask her, 'Do you feel like having something sour, puttar? I could ask my son to bring some tamarind.'

Moni never answered.

One afternoon, as Bebe sat in the turret with them, Soni asked her, 'Why do you always ask about something sour?'

'They say if there's great desire to have more and more sour things, the child will be a daughter. I never felt like having anything sour. Still, I'd send for the kamrakh and tamarind.'

'Why?'

'See, I gave birth to nine sons, and then these sons had sons too. The family has longed for a daughter. But we never had one.'

Bebe's voice choked. She rested her hand on Moni's shoulder and said, 'See, Moniye, if you have a daughter, she will be mine. I'll bring her up. I'll not snatch her from you, but I'll be her daadi. And if it's a boy, he'll be yours. I have one too many. You can then shower all your love on him.'

Bebe's eyes welled up as she said this, and she got up and walked away, tapping her chhadi on the ground. Moni was touched. For the first time, she stroked her belly and smiled. A wave of relief ran through Soni.

The Englishman Bebe had mentioned lived only twelve or fourteen miles away from Bundi. His house had been set on fire during the riots. Apparently, it was those rioters who had flown the saffron flag on the fort. The Englishman was an agriculturist. He owned some 125 acres of land in Alpha Nagar. His farmers and workers were joint owners of those lands. He himself had formulated those laws and followed them. When British rule was nearing its end, he declared himself a Hindustani. He demanded the right to become a citizen of Hindustan. People say he got up at night and rode his horse around his farms, like the kings of old times gathering news about their subjects. He loved his fields and crops.

But when the turmoil broke, his workers could not save him. His house, his possessions and cattle... he lost everything. He could not bear to see his fields on fire. Running through the flames, he burned himself to ashes.

After his death, the land became free but disputes erupted amongst the farmhands. They grabbed whatever land they could get their hands on, sold it and vanished. Punjab was not very far. Farmers and zamindars from Punjab bought the land.

Two of Bebe's sons bought a large part of the

land and became zamindars. They also took over the dilapidated old haveli in the middle of the fields and called Bebe over from Bundi fort.

When Bebe got the news, she hurried to the turret. Striking her stick on the floor, she said: 'The two of you will have to come with me.'

With the partition, a new system had emerged. Hiring houses by paying 'pagdi'. By depositing a pagdi at several places in the villages around the farms, Bebe's family began to settle down. She became the 'thakurain'. There were enough hands to sow the fields. Everyone found work. Bebe's sons managed to get a house for Soni and Moni as well.

No matter what Moni did or where she spent her time, she felt compelled to meet Bebe at least once a day. If Moni didn't go to her, Bebe would come.

'You will surely have a baby girl! The way you bang your left foot on the ground when you walk, you know…'

Inch by inch, Moni's womb was growing. When she felt irritable, she'd say to Soni, 'I'll sell her to some dalla.'

'Why not give her to Bebe if you don't want to bring her up?'

One reason they had come along with Bebe was that everyone had believed the lie about the child being her dead husband's. Now, it didn't matter what it looked like. Who had seen the man anyway?

Bebe would say, 'The girl will have her mother's looks. In fact, she will be more beautiful!'

The way Bebe stressed the word 'beautiful', it seemed as if it were predicted by a holy book. She laughed and said, 'She will be quite a handful for my grandsons!'

Bebe sat with Moni the whole night through when she went into labour. They had brought some haggard old midwife from a nearby village. She could hardly see, but her hands were strong and experienced.

Moni gave birth to a boy.

Bebe's heart sank. She said, barely suppressing a sob, 'Waheguru is still upset with me...'

Moni's breasts filled up with so much milk that

she forgot she was unmarried. She stared at her son as though he were a miracle. All the anger, disgust and hatred with which she would beat her belly were washed away. All the poison turned to nectar in her breasts.

Bebe visited frequently. Her love of the baby had not diminished even though it was a boy. She was not as well off as she used to be, but still brought a silver spoon for the boy.

'I'll organize the naming ceremony for your son at the gurudwara the moment the season's first seeds are sown.'

Different names were mentioned every day. One day Bebe asked Moni, 'What was your husband's name?'

Moni was caught unawares. She turned towards Soni, who blurted, 'Trilok … Trilok Singh!'

Bebe rattled off spontaneously, 'You can name the child "Trilok" … there, you've found all three worlds, that's what the word means!'

They didn't understand the meaning. But they nodded in agreement.

To everyone around, the boy was 'Loki'. He had a

heavy crop of hair and dark eyes. He looked nothing like Moni. But with his dense hair, he did look like a Trilok Singh.

As Loki grew older, everyone grew more attached to him. Moni and Soni used to work in the fields and Loki played through the day, with Bebe watching over him.

His hair grew longer and Bebe enjoyed plaiting it, tying it into a knot on his head. When he started walking, she would take him to the gurudwara too. She showed him off to her sons, who had cut their hair.

Once, Soni laughed and whispered in Moni's ear, 'Let's cut his hair. He'll get lice. All Sikhs do.'

Moni replied, amused, 'He is a Gur Sikh. Why should I cut his hair? If I did that, Bebe would cut my head off.'

But one day, she did something strange. She took the scissors and a comb and cut his hair. She kept combing, parting it this way and that. She stared hard at him. When Soni entered the room, Moni said: 'Soni, see! His face is like that one's ... doesn't he look exactly like the one who used to rape us every day?'

There was a strange madness in Moni's eyes. It scared Soni.

'Have you gone crazy? Move aside.' She picked Loki up and went out.

When Bebe saw the child, she turned her face away and wept. Soni reassured her, 'God knows what got into Moni. Don't cry, Bebe, the hair will grow back.'

'No, Soniye … my Waheguru is upset with me.'

After that day, Moni never came face-to-face with Bebe. But Soni noticed the deepening horror in her eyes. She found her sister staring at Loki like one possessed. The innocent child would call out, 'Ma … Ma…' and run towards her.

And then, one day, God's wrath fell.

They discovered Loki's body in the well. Moni was nowhere to be seen.

The police came and took Soni away. The senior inspector sahib wrote out the report, but Soni was not allowed to return home. He was sure that Soni's sister would come looking for her. He was right.

Three or four days later, some policemen caught hold of a hungry and distraught Moni. They brought her to the police station. Her eyes had the same madness.

Soni came to meet her, but Moni pushed her away. The policemen dragged her back to the cell. Soni could not stop sobbing.

The inspector released Soni. But where could she go? When she reached home, the whole of Alpha Nagar seemed alien. No one wanted to be seen with her. Bebe refused to meet her too. When she came back to the police station after two days, the inspector told her that Moni had been sent to Kota Central Jail. She was showing signs of being mentally ill.

With a dupatta on her head and wearing a pair of jootis, Soni somehow made it to Kota Central Jail.

A window-sized door opened within a colossal one. Guards were stationed on either side.

'I want to meet the jailor sahib,' Soni said.

'Why?'

'My sister is in jail here.'

'Do you have any order or a permit?'

No one would let her in. She stood waiting outside. Sometimes, she saw the jailor sahib's jeep come out or go in. She could only guess that he was the jailor. She would approach him, fold her hands and say, 'Salaam sahib.' He would simply drive past her. He had been seeing her there for a few days, resting against the wall, listless.

One day, he sent for her. The jailor sahib's living quarters were inside the jail. He had a servant in the house. Yusuf. His wife and children lived in Aligarh. When Soni came in, she again wished him with folded hands, 'Salaam sahib.' The jailor told her that whenever she called out 'Salaam sahib', he thought she was calling him by his name. He laughed. His name, he told her, was Abdul Salaam Quraishi. He sent Yusuf to bring her water and a meal. That evening, sitting in the lawn, he listened to her story. It was heart-rending.

Moni had been charged with murder. To allow her to meet Soni required clearance from senior officers.

'Salaam Sahib' took up the responsibility himself. He escorted Soni in his jeep.

Moni had been locked in an isolated cell. A woman constable went to inform her about her sister's visit, but she refused to see her.

'I don't want to meet her,' Moni said.

'She is standing outside.'

'Let her.'

Soni heard her.

The constable came out. Soni approached the cell and peeped inside through the bars. Moni was sitting against the wall. She turned to look at Soni. Then got up slowly and came to the door. The madness had not left her eyes.

'Moni, do you know what you have done?'

Moni spat out bitterly, 'Yes!' And then added: 'He killed so many Hindus in Campbellpur. So what if I have killed one small Musalman?'

PART THREE

Like dry leaves falling from a huge tree in a storm, the refugees kept drifting. At times they would float to the ground, only to be blown away by another strong gust of breeze.

Decades passed, the refugees kept wandering. It was impossible to say who moved where, fell where. Even time wouldn't probably be able to recognize them. The roots of the partition were buried deep, its branches reaching out. It was impossible to search for those who had left Campbellpur with Fauji. One leaf drifted a long way off.

'Papa, I'm ready to become a Hindu for Paul. I want to go to Hindustan, to see the place I was born in – Rajputana!'

For a moment George wondered if he too was a refugee from India. In England. He remembered Ramkumar Pushkarna of Rajputana. Jasmine too had stayed back.

George was quiet for a while. Then he said, 'I want you to get married in church. Don't embarrass me in front of my friends, Edna, the few who remain. Especially because the marriage is taking place here, in England. I'd have no objection if it were happening in Hindustan.'

Edna's father, George Samuel, had once lived in Hindustan. An official of the British administration, he had been honest, sociable and compassionate. He had been posted in Rajputana, where he had worked on building canals and wells. Shortage of water was the area's main problem. Particularly for the backward classes, who had to walk for miles to collect water. George would be touring for days, which irked his wife, Jasmine, especially in the last months of her pregnancy. There was no shortage of Hindustani servants, but she had no faith in their primitive ways. She wanted a doctor or trained nurse around at all times. But George trusted the experienced local midwives. He would say, 'Women here give birth every year. And these midwives help with one or two births every week without any modern equipment. They are expert hands.' Jasmine insisted on travelling with him, though it was dangerous to do so in her condition. But her husband was the top official of the region, and all possible arrangements were made. It was on one of those nights, near Pochina in Miyan Jaladh, that Edna was born. His only daughter.

In Hindustan, astrologers are wont to foretell one's fortunes. One day, when George was not home, an astrologer visited and mapped Edna's horoscope. 'Her name should start with the sound "aa". She will get married to a high-caste Brahmin.' The astrologer didn't know that she was Christian.

Government jobs are like a game of kho-kho. One rises, another sits, one goes, another comes. Soon after, George was stationed in Dera Ismail Khan as collector. The area was very different from Rajputana. Because George Samuel was a competent officer, he was always posted to problematic areas. At Dera Ismail Khan, there were problems with the

Pathans, who preferred to be called Pakhtoons. They had been sworn enemies of the Mughals whom they saw as invaders, like the British.

Despite all his preoccupations, George had a habit: keeping a diary. This is what made a philosopher of him over time. He was greatly impressed with Hindustani culture and philosophy. He developed a fondness for collecting folk stories and had read Lieutenant-Colonel James Tod's book on Rajputana.

About sixty miles away from Jaisalmer, in Khuri Gaon, lived a tribe of Manganiyar singers. This was a Muslim kabila, but their lifestyle was no different from that of Hindus. Their rituals and traditions were also similar. Although he was a good Christian, George believed that religion was a matter of personal choice. He felt that the culture of Hindustan transcended religious divides. Even if one were to change one's religion, the way of life would not.

When he was transferred to Dacca, his faith in this belief became stronger. In 1905, the British government had tried to divide Bengal on the basis of religion, and failed.

When he was posted in Dacca as culture deputy, a great change came over him. His attachment to Hindustan grew stronger. Along with the folk tales of Hindustan, he began to collect the baul songs of the area. He even started translating them into English.

During this phase, when he was collecting Lalan Fakir's baul songs, he met the renowned poet Qazi Nazrul Islam who wrote explosive poems and songs in defiance of British rule. He would even sing those songs.

George was impressed with Qazi sahib, the latter's hostility towards the British notwithstanding. Nazrul Islam wanted to translate the sacred book of Islam into Bangla verse. Many Muslims were upset with this attempt. That made him sad. He came to be known as the 'sad poet'.

George had started to speak some broken Bangla, and was very keen on the translation of the Quran Sharif. Some Musalmans suspected him of encouraging Qazi Nazrul to proceed with the translation. People hurled stones at his house, some even beat him up once or twice. The British government did not approve of George's approach to the issue, and sent him back to Rajputana. This time, under the culture ministry, he was given the task of building an opinion against sati amongst the people. In Bengal, thanks to the efforts of Raja Ram Mohan Roy, such a movement had already gained momentum.

As soon as he arrived in Rajputana, George began touring. He was on the lookout for someone who, like Lalan Fakir, was popular amongst the people and, like Raja Ram Mohan Roy, could stir a new movement. He found, instead, a fakir-like singer.

Ramkumar Pushkarna belonged to Kuldhara and was an itinerant singer of kathas. He was a pundit, his forehead smeared with tilaks. He was a learned shastri with the gift of the gab. Ramkumar could speak a bit of English and had very liberal ideas. He understood the need to put an end to the practice of sati.

One day, while George and he were returning from the burial of a friend, Ramkumar started to explain, 'See, George … Hindustan will never become Englistan. Ever. You people are not going to stay here forever. You'll have to go back. God forbid, if you die here, you will be buried in a grave … You will not be able to go back to your motherland. If your future generations sitting in Englistan remember you, you will appear foreign to them, and nobody will come to see you.'

George was listening attentively. He asked, 'So if one dies here, should one be cremated? The body burned?'

'Yes! That's exactly what I am saying. Not dust unto dust! Nature unto nature is the solution. Man emerged from nature, he has to return to it. Burn him and immerse the ashes in the river. He will reach the ocean. Collect the ashes and blow them into the fields. The earth will absorb them.'

'And the matter of rebirth? What happens after?'

'That is merely the greed to hold on to life! No one will rise from the tomb, or be born again.'

This stayed with George. He talked about it to Jasmine and decided to write it in his will.

But something else happened.

George was in Bikaner at the time of a smallpox outbreak. There was no cure for it then. The afflicted would wait for the epidemic to pass, leaving behind its marks. Or it would take you along. On its way out, it took Jasmine. Edna had a narrow escape.

George cremated his wife, instead of giving her a traditional Christian burial. He immersed her ashes in a canal so that she would be absorbed by the earth. It was an act that sparked outrage amongst the Christian community and led to heated debates in churches. After all, it was a matter of religion.

Hindustan resonated with passionate cries for freedom, while England was deeply involved in a world war. The British authorities thought it best to retire him.

George returned to England with Edna and settled in the suburban countryside of Coventry.

There, he continued to do what he loved. He collected folk tales and resumed writing. He also set up a small poultry farm.

The Second World War raged on. Nations burned in the furnace. By the time its fuel ran out, it had consumed people like Hitler. Statues of Stalin stood tall and Churchill's great empire began to crumble.

And all the while, George's poultry farm grew. He had no son he could entrust its management to. Though Edna was older now, there was little she could have done. George had seen women work in Hindustan, where they toiled in farms, ploughed land, ran shops and also pulled carts. It was unthinkable and unheard of in their society in England that women should engage in such manual work. No matter that they had a queen.

If he were business-minded, he would have hired a few extra hands. But of what use was that? All his needs were taken care of and he spent his time well, reading and writing. He would distribute the extra eggs in his neighbourhood.

Around the time that Edna was admitted into a college, another chunk of the Great Empire fell. Hindustan was partitioned. Once again, George said, 'Impossible! That country cannot be divided on the basis of religion. Their culture is ancient. Enduring.'

'But it's true, Papa. There is a Pakistan now.'

'It will not hold. Punjab, Bengal, the Pathan culture – they are far too different from one another. No religion will bind them.'

People flocked to England from both parts of the newly divided country. They came searching for work and shelter. Here, they could greet each other like long-lost brothers. They belonged neither to Hindustan nor Pakistan. They had a common name: refugees.

An impoverished young man was admitted to Edna's college. He was a Hindu, but Pakistani, and a refugee.

He was quite thin and had a pale face. His jaw kept moving as if he was biting his teeth. He was a shy boy, rather nervous. Edna quite liked him. One day, she approached him, asking his age.

'Satarah ... Seventeen.'

He was two years younger than her.

When Edna offered him a ride on her bicycle once, he refused.

'Scared?' she asked.

He shook his head. 'No.'

'Well then, you ride it and I will sit at the back.'

He agreed, and soon she learnt his name. Jaipal.

Edna took him to her father's farm and introduced him to George.

George asked, 'Where are you from?'

'Campbellpur.'

'Attock, boy. That's what Campbellpur's real name is.' George had seen the place. He continued, 'And from where in Attock?'

Jaipal tried to describe the location with an address and some landmarks, but George knew only the name of a school there. 'I know of M.B. Middle School. Station Road.'

All at once, Jaipal felt that he was meeting someone from his motherland. Immediately, he touched George's feet.

'What are you doing?' Edna exclaimed.

George embraced him and replied, 'This is Hindustani culture, Edna.'

Jaipal had already shifted three houses in Southall. He would wake up early, sweep the house, wash the dishes and rush to college. He found a place to stay at the YMCA for two months. Lodgings were free but he had no income and had exhausted his savings. He struggled to pay the tuition fee. Whenever it comes, poverty peeps through one's clothes. Edna noticed it and bought him a jacket. It may have covered his back, but could not fill his belly. Hunger showed on his face. He began to miss lectures. When his name was about to be struck off the rolls, Edna forced him onto the back of her bicycle and brought him to her father.

George offered some immediate help. But as a good administrator, he also found a long-term solution to the problem. He gave Jaipal a place to stay on his poultry farm, and let him sell the extra eggs. This became a steady source of income for Jaipal. Familiar with the households of Southall, he would go door-to-door selling eggs. As his income grew, he used part of it on the upkeep of the farm.

Jaipal's education too diversified. In college he used to study history; here he took up books on bird breeding. George had never been obsessed with his poultry farm. He was surprised to see Jaipal's passion for the hens. It also fanned Edna's interest in the birds. Gradually, Samuel Poultry Farm became a household name.

Unfortunately, Jaipal's formal education suffered as the business flourished. Some people who had come from Pakistan had constructed small shacks and shops in the era. Samuel Poultry Farm supplied not only eggs but also chicken to these. Ironically enough, the question of 'halal-haram' was rendered immaterial. The refugees had found their refuge. Pal became Paul, the pronunciation just as anglicized.

The sun was beginning to set on the British Empire. There was pressure on the island. Taxes were on the rise, and efforts were being made to reduce the number of foreigners. New passports became difficult to acquire. The situation changed for refugees from India and Pakistan. Everyone began to devise strategies to stay there. Some even married white women to acquire citizenship. Religion and names began to change. When discussing the matter at Samuel Poultry Farm, George asked Paul about his passport.

When Paul did not answer, George repeated, 'Passport! Where is it?'

'I don't have one, sir!' Paul replied.

'How did you come to England?'

'On a cargo ship. I had a false passport, some

Mohammad Anvar's. I got a haircut of the same style and came. I ran away from the docks … and tore up the passport. Many people arrive like this – there are agents who arrange it.'

George was shocked. Why had he not enquired earlier?

'What about college?'

'Bribe, sir … it's a long story. I came here to study. But … Edna knows it all, sir. I told her everything. I wanted to tell you, but Edna stopped me, sir!'

George fell silent. He sighed and got to his feet. Pouring himself a drink, he said, 'Get married here and apply for a British passport. You are no longer a refugee – not after having worked here for so many years. You are a British citizen. I will give you a permit.'

'Sir … I wish to marry Edi.'

George's eyes darted to Edna who was standing near the door.

'Yes,' she said at length. 'I am ready to become a Hindu, Papa … I must go to Hindustan, see the place where I was born – Rajputana.' She paused and then said, 'If Mother had had a grave there, I would have visited it for her blessing.'

It had crossed George's mind that Edna and Paul were in a relationship. He said, 'I want you to get married in church. Don't embarrass me in front of my friends, Edna, the few who remain. Especially because the marriage is taking place here, in England. I'd have no objection if it were happening in Hindustan.'

Edna asked, 'Can we go to Hindustan for our honeymoon?'

Paul replied, 'But I am from Pakistan. I was a Pakistani refugee in India. I don't know India beyond some refugee camps. But I can take you to Campbellpur—'

George stopped him: 'Attock, beta, Attock, not Campbellpur! You do not have to be a Hindu to belong to Hindustan. Or even Pakistan or Britain for that matter. But take her to Rajputana once – they call it Rajasthan now.'

'But, sir, I love Campbellpur!'

'Attock!' Walking slowly, he came closer to both of them.

'You have my blessings! Mubarak ho! Cheers,' he said, raising a toast to them.

The years rolled by. But the refugees were far from settled. They were trying to. The handful of passengers who had left Campbellpur with Fauji were still searching for their soil. They were still rootless.

Paul may have forgotten Hindustan, but George could not. In 1962, when India and China were at war, he explained, 'See, this is Pakistan's war. They want Kashmir. They are preparing for that with China.' He went on, 'They want to assess Hindustan's military power and leave it vulnerable.'

He was now sixty-four and had a two-year-old grandson, Peter Paul. One day, when George took Peter out in a pram, someone came to Samuel Poultry Farm. He was the owner of Fazal Food

Centre and hailed from Attock. George was intrigued and brought him home to meet Paul.

When Paul spoke to him in Punjabi, the man embraced him. His name was Saleem Siddique and he owned a small Pakistani-style eatery for kababs, Fazal Food Centre.

'Ekdum dhaba style! Now I want to start a canned-food business.' He added in a low voice, 'To tell you the truth, I am looking for a partner. I have heard a lot about your poultry farm and assumed it was run by an angrez. Thought I should see for myself. And look! I have found an Indian brother!'

'I'm Pakistani. And as Dad must have told you, I am from your town, Campbellpur!'

'Now they call it Attock.'

Soon after the introductions, Paul opened his heart to him.

'I want to take my wife to Pakistan.'

'Whenever you say. It's summer now. Let's go in the winter, when we can eat to our heart's content.'

'Is Gurudwara Road still there?'

'Ji, of course it is! And it's still called Gurudwara Road.'

'And Ghantaghar Chowk?'

'That too. The old clock was vandalized. The replacement has been working fine though.'

Paul's eyes grew misty. He asked, 'You have a family there?'

'There's my wife and two-three children.' He laughed. 'I mean two. The third is on its way.'

'Who else?'

'I have a brother in Dubai. He has a good business there.'

'Is Fazal Food Centre named after him? You are Saleem Ahmed.'

'No, no, Fazal is my father, Master Fazaldeen Siddique.'

'I see. What does he do?'

'He is no more. He used to teach … was the headmaster of a school. I'll show you his school too. There's a new building there. At one time, it was just a middle school. Now, it has grown into a college. Pakistan has progressed a lot.'

That winter, Paul went to his beloved Campbellpur. Edna did not accompany him. She wanted to go to Rajputana.

Paul looked up at the Ghantaghar. In the winter fog, it looked like a work of art. The old British-style spire on top captivated him. The same style had never appealed to him in Britain.

Saleem took him home. They were business partners now, heading Eastern Canned Food. His house was in a new area within the city; a new, two-storeyed building. This was in the name of both the brothers, Siddique House. Inside, in the hall, hung a large portrait of Fazaldeen Siddique.

Saleem said, 'This enlargement was made in England. Photography had yet to catch on here. When the middle school was demolished for reconstruction, a clerk found the photo in a register and brought it to me. He also gave me the photograph of a Sardar, my father's friend. I forget his name. We were very young then. He visited us often. I remember something very interesting about him. Sardar-ji had tied his buffalo to our door just before he left for India. On its back, written with chalk, were the words: "I'm leaving Pakistan in your custody."'

Both laughed. 'He was a schoolmaster, after all. Was used to writing on a blackboard!' Saleem said. 'Where was your house?'

'In Civil Lines.'

'Oh ho ... Now there are government offices there.'

'I went around looking for it yesterday. Could not even recognize the road,' Paul confessed.

The next day, Paul took Saleem along and finally found the place. The kothi's front and back had flipped over. At its rear, a big broad road had been built ... this was the main road now. Where there had been the front lawn, a wall had been raised and a six-storeyed government building had come up. The house sat dwarfed between two buildings.

After some enquiries, they found a way in. A muhajir family lived there now. They were cultured people. Many rooms within rooms had been constructed. They were invited in and served tea and homemade gajar ka halwa.

Paul grew tearful. 'In those days, this house seemed so big.'

The master of the house responded sensitively, 'I'm sure it was, janab. The tall buildings around it make it look smaller. Also, you are taller now, the doors must look small to you. You must have been very young when you lived here.'

'Ji.'

Paul could not stay any longer. He was ready to leave.

As he was getting up, Ali Raza sahib said, 'We have something for you in our safekeeping. I hoped someone, someday, would return for it.'

He fetched something wrapped in old crinkled paper. It was a marble plate. He said, 'This must have been part of the front gate. There's none now. But…'

Paul unwrapped it. On top of it, in English, was the address:

Rai Bahadur Des Raj
Kothi No. 8
Civil Lines
Campbellpur

Paul broke down. He sat down, hugging the plate to his chest, and sobbed.

'This is my father.' His father's face rose in front of him. A golden kulla wrapped in a Pathani turban. How royal he looked. Even in the truck, he had asked for the keys to the kothi. He must have hoped to return someday.

George was right. The divisions wrought by religion never lasted. The '60s had just wound down when Pakistan broke up. A part of it became a new nation. Bangladesh.

Another strong gust of wind started blowing dry leaves all over. Another decade passed. The '70s.

Some leaves from Fauji's truck had just found their soil and had started to grow in a new land, when another storm arose...

It was a ball of fire that started from Delhi and spread with such speed that it engulfed large parts of India within hours.

Mobs moved around in all directions with sticks, swords and axes. They would identify Sikhs by their turbans and beards and pick them out like insects in wheat. Hunt for them in markets, shops, houses and colonies. They stopped trains and dragged them out. Then, they shaved their heads. Like Muslims had forcefully circumcised Hindu men during the partition.

The prime minister of India, Indira Gandhi, had been assassinated by her Sikh bodyguard in Delhi.

Kartar Singh had come to Kanpur. His son had cut his hair despite being a Gur Sikh. He was unhappy about it. After disowning his son, he had spent the night in a gurudwara. In the morning, he was about to leave for Delhi when he heard the news of the assassination. He also heard that anti-Sikh riots had erupted in Delhi.

He had left his wife and mother behind and was worried about their safety. Outside the railway station, he saw a mob. They were pulling some Sikhs by their hair and dragging them out of the station, raising slogans.

'*Khoon ka badla khoon se lenge!*'

Baffled, he turned around. A Miyan slapped his turban away and said in a suppressed voice: '*O Sikkha, marega!*'

The stranger pushed him into his truck and raised the plank at the back. Kartar's head was spinning. Before he could gather his senses, Miyan-ji quickly started the truck and drove off. Kartar kept rolling from side to side in the empty truck as they moved on.

On the highway, Jafar Miyan stopped the truck at a lonely spot and rebuked him. 'You're lucky! Don't you know what's going on out there?'

He asked Kartar to come out of the back and sit in the front, next to him. They started again. He briefed Kartar about what was happening.

'Don't take the train under any circumstances. Trains are being stopped and Sikhs massacred. They are burning shops owned by Sikhs.' He paused, before continuing, 'Where were you headed?'

'Delhi.'

'What do you do in Delhi?'

Kartar responded, voice quivering, 'I have a shop selling auto parts.'

'Hope there's no khanda on your signboard?'

'No! But it says ... Singh Auto Parts.'

A long silence and then suddenly Miyan-ji asked, 'Shall I cut your hair? It will grow back.'

Kartar's hand went straight to his head.

'Don't worry, it was only a suggestion for your safety. I respect sardars. I have sardar friends. I am going in the same direction. Karnal. I will drop you off somewhere.'

Jafar Miyan was a patient man, experienced in the ways of the world. He had seen the country through its many ups and downs. He narrated an experience. 'If a Sikh had not given us refuge, we'd have gone to Pakistan. When riots broke out in Delhi in 1947, Sardar Patel made arrangements for Muslims who wanted to go to Pakistan. Camps were put up in Purana Qila. From there they would be escorted by the military across the border. Our family also took refuge in the qila. My father's bosom school friend, Sardul Singh, came to know of that. He searched for us and found us in the camp. He beseeched my father and took us home under military security. He was a very influential man. Our Abba too was a Congressi. We stayed back in India.

'Till such time as Nehru was alive, our Abba had no fear. But after his death ... well, it was a different matter. My father used to say, "One can never tell when the pot might boil over in this country. Politics here is like the hookah of the village chaupal. Whoever has the pipe becomes a zamindar."'

Jafar Miyan knew more than he let on.

He paused for a bit and said, 'The country will keep breaking and uniting. It's a centuries-old habit of our rulers. Some outsider may come and unite us, but we will never do it on our own. For that, you need to learn about democracy.'

'How do you know all this?'

'Abba used to tell us. I told you, he was with the Congress.' He sighed and continued, 'Amma-Abba are no more. But I do have an elder brother. He went away to America. He is doing well. I could have gone too, but I never felt like leaving Hindustan.' He paused again. 'There's something about its air – we remain attached to it and yet distant.'

'Why? Don't you ever get fed up of the riots?'

Jafar Miyan took a long breath and said, 'It's like this, Kartar. Those who didn't want to migrate to Pakistan, but were forced to, looked to the West. It was the same for those who didn't want to come here from Pakistan, but had to. They too seized the first opportunity and left. That's why, when they meet each other abroad, they meet with great love … like long-lost lovers. They have enough sorrows to share.'

Kartar Singh said, 'I feel the same sometimes, but … I cannot leave my mother and go. If it weren't for her … I would have perished in some refugee camp.'

Jafar Miyan asked, 'You too have come from the other side?'

'Yes, we crossed over in a truck like yours.'

A deep silence descended upon them. Only the sound of truck wheels on the tar road could be heard.

Jafar Miyan said, 'I have a suggestion – tie your hair at the back and wear your turban around your neck like fakirs do. Then, as long as you're with me, people will not take you for a Sikh. Tomorrow morning I will drop you near Dhaula Kuan and leave for Karnal. I don't have a permit for Delhi. Inshallah, this fire too will die down in a day or two.'

Jafar Miyan stopped at a dhaba or two he knew on the way. But the same news was aflame everywhere. Some abandoned trucks could be seen. Must have belonged to Sikhs. They drove all night without a wink of sleep.

When they reached Delhi, the sun had risen. But what they saw as they entered was enough to shock them. As soon as they turned towards Munirka, they saw a mob dragging a Sikh towards an electric pole to which another Sikh was already tied. A burning tyre hung around his neck. Dense smoke rose all around. The second one was screaming with all his might, 'Don't kill me. Don't kill … Indira was my mother. Don't kill me.'

Jafar Miyan turned the truck in another direction. There was no sign of the police anywhere. Kartar's voice trembled as he said, 'This has been happening since yesterday. By now, the military should have intervened, but even the police aren't here.'

'They won't come,' Jafar Miyan said coolly. Then, in a gentle voice he added, 'Come with me, Kartar. We will go to Karnal.'

'No, no, Miyan-ji. My mother will die of worry and grief. Leave me at the next turning from Dhaula Kuan. My shop is not far from there. I'll make a phone call home.'

'Even the shop will not be safe, Kartar!'

TWO

'I … I will lock the door from the inside. I will take the signboard off.'

Jafar Miyan kept driving.

Kartar never got a chance to take off the signboard. The mob had arrived. He had fastened the iron shutter. Holding the iron rod of the roshandan, Kartar trembled uncontrollably. Thank God he had fixed cardboard on the roshandan whose glass was broken. A crowd had gathered outside his shop. They were screaming, 'Come out, oye Sikkha! Come out!'

They were unable to break open the shutter. When they pushed hard, it rattled, offering Kartar a glimpse of the scene outside.

The tyres heaped outside were being looted. Kartar knew how they planned to use them. He had seen it only this morning. Two Sikhs had been dragged by their turbans and tied to electric poles. The tyres were hurled around their necks and petrol sprinkled on them. Then they were set on fire. Their screams would have been heard all the way to Defence Colony. And then died down in the smoke.

There were a number of people in khadi egging on the mob.

Some 'patriot' shouted, 'Oye, break the rear wall!'

Kartar jumped out through the roshandan and dashed across a back lane. His turban came off. His hair fell loose. He thought of stopping somewhere and cutting it off.

Then he remembered. How he had disowned his son for the same act.

Somewhere in his heart, he felt relief. Poor fellow, my son at least will be safe now. He clung to the walls and tried to find a place to hide. As he turned into another lane, he saw some people trying to set fire to a house. They were hurling petrol-soaked fireballs through its windows. The slogans were the same: 'Come out, Sikkha. Come out!'

People were armed with sticks. They held axes and some brought tyres, rolling them along. He slipped into another lane.

There was yet another mob up ahead. Where had all these people come from? There were villagers among them. Young people and old. Bodies still burned against some lamp-posts. Black tresses of smoke rose into the sky.

Delhi had gone mad.

Yes, he did know that some Sikh had killed the prime minister.

But Gandhi had been killed by a Hindu. So?

Where was the police? The military?

Suddenly, some people saw him and screamed. 'There ... a Sikh!'

He ran as he had never run before. He sprinted through the lanes as if he were jumping across canals. He started to pant. Screaming voices followed him. He came to a dead end. A garbage van stood in the corner. He plunged headlong into the garbage. The angry voices grew louder, closer. Then, gradually, they faded away.

Twenty-four hours had passed since he had jumped into the pile of garbage. He had spent a day and night in the same way in a haystack once, when his father and mother were killed in front of him. He was very young and Baba, his grandfather, had carried him to the cowshed. He had hidden him in a haystack and warned him against even breathing too loud. He was yet to overcome the fear that took root in him that day. The haystack could have been set on fire any time. The next day, when his Baba had taken him out of the stack, a truck driver had offered them a ride. He was coming to Hindustan.

Baba had urinated in the truck, he suddenly remembered. Scared, he felt his pyjamas and found they were wet. He could smell nothing because he was covered in filth. How long had he been here? A day ... two days ... four days? His hands and legs had become numb. His head was spinning, or had the garbage van begun to move? Where was it headed? Would it leave him in the same wilderness he had left his Baba? Would he find his Maiyya there again?

Maiyya ... Panna Maiyya ... she will manage to find me in this wilderness. He was becoming delirious.

Panna had been sitting at the threshold for three days.

'Kartara has not come!'

Kartar's wife, Jaswant Kaur, reassured her, 'He'll come, Maiyya. Good that he went off to Kanpur. It saved him.'

'The Musalmans must have burned down the shop.'

'Not Musalmans, Maiyya … these are Hindus.'

Jassi coaxed and persuaded Maiyya indoors. There was only one way to keep her occupied: start off with some old memory. Maiyya would be distracted narrating it.

'Maiyya, you came right up to Dilli with the refugees. Why didn't you settle down?'

'I did, beti. One doesn't always settle down with a husband. Mothers can settle down with their sons too. And why a son? Kartara was like my grandson … he was that young. You were not even born then!'

Jassi laughed. 'And that … Fauji … if only he had come with you.'

Panna sighed and fell silent for a while. 'That night in the ruins was very lonely, Jassi. He had even suggested going back … But as soon as it was morning, Kartara made the decision for me. If his grandfather hadn't died … I don't know…' She shrugged.

Jassi said, 'Maiyya, do you feel Fauji thinks of you?'

A faint smile spread across Panna's face. 'Hmm…
I think of him, he must also be thinking of me.
When I was descending the mountain, I turned to
look once. He was going down the other side.'

Jassi asked, 'He was older than you, na?' She
paused. 'Could he still be alive?'

That faint smile remained as Panna answered, 'I
am alive, he must be too.'

He is over ninety years old. He has lost all the hair on his head, apart from two strands on the sides. When these stray into his mouth, he wets his fingers with his spit and pulls them back into place. His eyes still shine the way they did. Flaming torches. Even today, he roams the Valley of Kashmir like a fakir.

Fauji is still alive.

In 1947, coming down the mountain, he had joined a caravan. Had gone some way with it. He thought of Lakhbeera and the dhaba. It dawned on him that there would be nothing there. No one. Why go back then? He stopped and looked back. In the direction Panna had gone.

Suddenly, he thought of his mother. She must be

in Jaunpur. Should he go? See her? Would she have started for Rawalpindi again? Could she be in this very caravan? Uff!

He moved away from the caravan.

What sort of a fall is this? People were still falling like autumn leaves … Drifting around like dry leaves.

That's where he left the caravan and started on a pagdandi alone. Wherever it went. Wherever it took him.

Fauji kept walking. Endless days. Infinite nights.

He spent fifty long years walking the pagdandis of Kashmir. The Valley too had been divided. Uff! These partitions never end. He did not know which side he was on.

He lives in a graveyard with a gravedigger. Now he knows where he has to go. The last address is not far from his room.

History marched on to complete another century. It was 1999. It was Kargil. The night kept resounding with explosions and gunfire.

Lying in his room in the graveyard, Fauji turned over and muttered, 'There they go again, the rascals! They didn't let me sleep all night.'

These wars were not new for him. Nor were the soldiers. They were like schoolboys, scaring each other, wearing borrowed masks. One throws a brick, the other hurls a stone. They keep sharpening their nails to lunge at each other.

'Fifty years ... in fact, more. God knows when they will grow up,' he muttered.

In the morning, he picked up his potli and stuffed his chillum. Then he took to the pagdandi towards the basti:

Painde lambe ne lakiran de
Umr de hisaab muk gaye
Totey labbe taqdiran de
Kisse lambe ne lakiran de

Long are the passages of borders
One has lost count of age
Gathering the pieces of fate
Long are the stories of the partition...

A NOTE ON *TWO*

P.S.

**Insights,
Interviews &
More...**

Of late, in the context of the seventieth year of our independence, it has been a revelation to hear people mention the Partition in the same breath as Independence. In fact, if anything, the reference to the Partition, separation, has been more pronounced than to Independence. Unlike, say, the horrors of the Holocaust or the Second World War, which have now become history, the Partition continues to be part of our social-political discourse. This may be because the War has found an outlet in the arts, in the books that have been written on it, in the films that have addressed its horrors. We, on the other hand, have had very little discussion around the Partition. Like a family secret which everyone knows of but is uncomfortable to talk about, we have pulled a curtain over it. It continues to fester.

Two addresses this work-in-progress nature of the cataclysmic events of 1947. A group of refugees starts out from Campbellpur/Attock in the winter of 1946. They make their way to the border. But what next? The passage to the border is not an end. It is what follows that lends their journey the nature of an odyssey, one that has not stopped. Uprooted from the only place they knew as their home, these refugees, and millions like them, have kept travelling, physically and metaphorically, in search of roots, in search of a place called home.

This is a work of fiction, but the characters who inhabit it and the experiences they go through are not. They are the result of my imagination working on the people I have known, the stories they have shared. The boy who runs away from home, boards a truck and works at a dhaba and as a cleaner. The Englishman after whom Alpha Nagar is named. The Rai Bahadur who, making his way to the border as a refugee, asks his wife, 'Hope you didn't leave the keys of the kothi at the chowk.' The owner of the canned food business in the UK. And, of course, the riots of 1984, the war in Kargil. These are people and events I have known, have lived through. I have used their stories and given them an imaginative spin as a storyteller. No work of fiction exists in a vacuum. Mine too is rooted in the world I have seen and experienced.

People who have read drafts of the book have termed it a novella, as my first attempt at long-form fiction. I am not sure what to say. For me, it is a novel; it has an arc of its own that has a beginning and which makes its way to an open end. The length is immaterial. It is what I needed to tell the story. When I can say what I have to in a few lines, I do it through my poems. When a few more sentences and paragraphs are needed, I fall back on the short story. The people I encounter in *Two*, the journeys they make, needed a little more elaboration than was possible in a poem or a short story. That is what dictated the form and the length. The rest is all for academics to debate.

GULZAR